I0521321

Storylandia

The Wapshott Journal of Fiction

Issue 14

The Wapshott Press

Storylandia, Issue 14, The Wapshott Journal of Fiction, ISSN 1947-5349, ISBN 978-0-9884093-2-3, is published at intervals by the Wapshott Press, PO Box 31513, Los Angeles, California, 90031-0513, telephone 323-201-7147. All correspondence can be sent The Wapshott Press, PO Box 31513, LA CA 90031-0513. Visit our website at www.WapshottPress.com This work is copyright © 2014 by Storylandia. The Wapshott Journal of Fiction, Los Angeles, California. "Dead End" is copyright © 2014 Chad Denton and is reprinted here with the copyright owner's permission. Copyright for the cover artwork is held by the artist and is reprinted here under the Creative Commons Attribution 2.0 Generic license.

Storylandia is always seeking quality original short stories, novelettes, and novellas. Please have a look at our submission guidelines at www.Storylandia.WapshottPress.com or email the editor at editor@wapshottpress.com

Many thanks to Kathleen Warner for the proofread and editorial support.

Cover: "City on the Edge," by Michael Day, http://commons.wikimedia.org/wiki/File:City_on_the_edge_%286647182351%29.jpg

Storylandia

The Wapshott Journal of Fiction

Founded in 2009

Issue 14, Autumn 2014

Edited by Ginger Mayerson

Table of Contents

Dead End   1
    Chad Denton

Chad Denton

Dead End

AUTHOR'S PREFACE

Joy Chevern and Rodney Bauman. Their names have been and still are a staple of TV news, talk shows, blogs, and the information networks of both the left and right wings. Writers of made-for-TV movies and PhD theses have all tried to lock down their motives. The only conclusion would-be scholars and Hollywood's dregs can agree on is that Rodney and Joy have managed to force the entire world to redefine crime and culture.

This is a risky statement to make at the start of such a book, but I honestly do not know if I have anything new to offer the nation's conversations on who these people were and what their crimes mean for the future. Instead my only goal is to attempt to pierce the mind of Rodney Bauman, using everything I could piece together from records, interviews, and other sources. With *Dead End*, I am not trying to make yet another entertainment commodity out of their notoriety, but rather, in spite of my lack of a graduate degree, to make an academic effort to simply understand *why*. This may seem like a thankless and perhaps even pointless quest, but I have been fortunate enough to enjoy the full cooperation of Bauman himself and the people who know him.

1

"I want to be famous." When he was a child, these were the only words Rodney had in mind whenever a teacher or relative would deploy the dreaded "What do you want to be?" question.

Rodney tightly held on to that answer through his childhood, even though he had learned by experience that "What do you want to be famous *for*?" would follow.

To that inquiry, he had no reply, stock or otherwise. How was he supposed to know why and how this ambition crawled its way into his very being like starving bacteria? The exact moment of infection was a perfect mystery even to him. Yes, his parents had the standard issue 9-5 office jobs, which slowly seeped like a poison fog into every aspect of their lives smothering books and politics and vacations as viable topics of conversation, but it was not only all that. The dull anxiety that he might have to share in their fate—auctioning off the better slice of his life just to help make a handful of rich people he'll never meet slightly richer—only kept the disease nourished.

He actually pitied his peers who squealed to anyone within earshot that they wanted to be policemen and firemen and doctors. Rodney was precociously beyond such things. Policemen and firemen and doctors never become famous, Rodney instinctively knew early on, unless they mess up or go crazy and kill somebody, and not always even then. He only had respect to spare for the occasional quiet, pompous kid who, with the sort of rabid confidence that can only spring from a near total absence of self-esteem, would declare that they wanted to be President. For the most part, Presidents, especially the Nixons, all have guaranteed fame.

There was one little problem that threatened to damn Rodney: there was absolutely nothing remotely exceptional about him. He kept noticing this rupture in the grand design since that apocalyptic December evening when he forgot half his lines and dropped the other half like dumbbells during Ms. Deming's eighth-grade production of *We've Always Lived in This Castle*. Since first grade he was a clockwork B-C student, too much of a fuck-up to crack even the lower ranks of the preppy academic aristocracy while too terrified of punishment to dive into the colorful delinquent community. Nor was he a natural leader. Long ago, he resigned himself to the inescapable fact that in classes and for the rest of his life he would only surrender his opinion when attacked head-on by the natural alpha human. In fact, if he ever did have a truly useful talent, it was detecting with fine canine senses the faintest trace of coming responsibility and escaping from its unwholesome presence.

Rodney could not sing—it was beyond him much the same way nuclear physics is beyond a cat— and lacked the patience to even try to tame a musical instrument. Besides, just thinking of performing in front of a crowd only made him envision rioters in the French Revolution gleefully popping off heads like bottle caps. Athletics was simply not an option, most of all because hours of grueling, self-inflicted physical torture seemed too high a price to pay.

Having no knack for humor, he was totally dependent on overspiced sex jokes and glib lines cribbed from late night sitcoms to stay interesting to his friends. Ideas for stories and novels eluded him or ended up resembling whatever he last read and liked to the point of artless plagiarism. Several times in junior high he did dedicate his life toward becoming a filmmaker, but for all his trouble only earned the requisite promises of support from the adults who must have felt they had the obligation to do so in any case, at least until the next faddish dream came along.

The most backing in his life plan Rodney ever received was not from his parents or relatives or friends, but from the small city that had been his home all through childhood. Named Dead End as if part of an elaborate practical joke, the city once had a reputation as an economic and social hub back when Adolf Hitler was still just an international eccentric, but it had never quite recovered from a post-Eisenhower economic downturn. The scars were still visible in the form of abandoned office buildings and department stores, still bearing on their faded bricks the ghost-gray imprints from their 1950s signs. The occasional restaurant or antique store would appear on the first floors of these buildings, feeding selfishly on the commercial carcasses like maggots, until their own brief two-year-at-most lifespan was finished. Once the name of Dead End actually was an earnest description: during the early nineteenth century, when the city was developing, a major highway that once winded through the state abruptly stopped there, but Rodney's eighth-grade English teacher always insisted that the name really came from the newborn city's exceptionally high suicide rate.

The terminally humorless always pushed to

change the name. Their natural leader was the local evangelical, the Rev. Lou Meredith, who had capped off a career built on the backs of the perpetually offended by opening up the ostentatiously named Patriot University, an institution of higher learning for those who didn't believe in institutions of higher learning. Rev. Meredith reigned from up high like a feudal magnate, gently yet righteously encouraging theater owners not to screen films that failed to pass the most rigorous cultural and political screening tests and intervening from time to time to stop the city from evolving anything that resembled a halfway decent night life. The only bars tolerated were in brand-name chain restaurants. For Rodney, the Dante-esque price of failing to even get a slight grip on a fame-making career would be a life spent back there, under a regime as harsh as it was bland.

By the time he entered high school, the expected teenage anxieties, even the inconvenience of realizing that he was gay, were all drowned out by the horror, growing fatter year by year, that he would have to live forever with this particular itch. Luckily, he found himself on the road to Damascus during his junior year in high school, seventeen minutes into Algebra II class. Motivated by a higher force than adolescent ennui, Rodney began assessing himself in his notebook with the penetrating efficiency of a bureaucratic agency, taking careful stock of his skills and his flaws. Most importantly he realized that he was: 1) a slightly-above-average writer, 2) somewhat skilled at pestering people who didn't want to talk to him, and 3) exceptional at pleasing authority figures and kowtowing before authorities and those at the top of his school's caste system. His final conclusion was only the first step: he would work to become a famous

American journalist.

From there and into his college years, Rodney could walk with the confidence that at one time he feared he would never know. He even shocked himself by actually being quite good at this vocation while paying dues at the university newspaper. Interviewees were disarmed by the casual bashfulness Rodney retained from childhood and were quite often deluded into believing that they were volunteering information as a personal favor. With surgical expertise he cut out fragments of information from the longest and most tedious of meetings and speeches, the only useful skill school had perfected in him. Soon enough Rodney wrapped himself every day in fantasies of future interviews with the most influential of politicians and the most worthless of celebrities. Most precious and thrilling were the waking dreams where he himself was interviewed; his own opinions, no matter how trivial or absurd or objectively false, were written down and processed for mass consumption. Such daydreams crowded out his occasional and trifling fantasies of love and sex (but mostly sex) by roughly a five to one ratio.

On one level Rodney knew that he was naïve to anticipate such success, an unpleasant reminder enforced by the old adults in his life who talked from their scripts about the "real world," but on another he felt it was as simple as any true matter of justice. Although he never really spent any real thoughts toward God's existence or lack thereof, he sometimes entertained the idea that the universe was so much more than just the end result of a series of cosmic accidents. Sometimes he even felt deep to his core that whatever the driving force of existence was, it would never be so petty as to give him an appetite that could never be satisfied. "But would it?" he often asked himself in those rare nightmarish moments he felt the whim to be philosophical. To him, all of human history seemed to contain nothing more interesting or profound than the fact that the universe had nothing consistent about it except a dark sense of humor.

It was when he spent the first two months after graduation failing to even be called in for one job interview that his nascent faith in a kind, guiding hand began to wither. Raking together what money he could, Rodney moved to New York City, finding a two-room basement apartment that custom-fit his Spartan needs. He only really cared about having enough money to eat reasonably well or at least to offset his inability to cook and to buy books and DVDs every now and then. Above him lived a 38-year old bookkeeper, Geoff, and his 27-year old boyfriend, Hans, an aspiring director from Switzerland, who fought so violently that the vision of being a witness at a murder trial bubbled in Rodney's mind more than once. As he found himself relying on temp jobs, each one more like twenty-first century serfdom than the last, Rodney began to increasingly see the appeal of a nervous breakdown and the accompanying excuse to rest.

As if he sniffed the emotional and spiritual burdens of another would-be somebody, Hans had gotten into the habit of bringing down his own experiments in fusing international cuisines, not all of which were tests in gastronomic endurance. Hans, who had a build that could quite possibly discourage muggers and a Germanic air that could be complimented as authentically pagan, seemed to Rodney criminally wasted on Geoff, an unexciting specimen of the species of thin, extraordinarily-average-looking-but-very-well-dressed urban professional that swarmed over

New York City. During his second visit Rodney learned that Hans was a fellow traveler, who loved the concept of cinema but loved the dream of seeing his name in a magazine he could pick up at any newsstand on any given Manhattan street even more.

On a Saturday when Geoff was out of town, Hans visited for the first time without an offering of food. For almost the entire time they talked not about the expected topics, like Hans's undead relationship with Geoff or Rodney's own lack of substantial dating credentials, but instead they mourned the faltering of each others' dreams, bitterly remonstrating against the refusal of the outside world to be even slightly reasonable. Rodney raged against Time-Warner for never giving him an interview, even for an entry-level desk job. Hans talked about how during his day job, directing episodes of *The Young and the Restless*, he still spent a good part of his time laying out blueprints for what he hopes will be his first feature-length film: a re-imagining of *Othello* that takes place within a small community of transsexual prostitutes in a post-apocalyptic Los Angeles.

It was after describing how Iago turns out to be an uptight undercover cop working for a Neo-Fascist cult/government that Hans innocuously positioned his hand just over Hans's knee. From there, with such an inevitability that Rodney felt like a peeping Tom to his own sexual adventure, came the deep silence, then the eye contact, next the leaning in, and finally contact. So Rodney, who was accustomed to thinking of sex as merely a hypothetical, lost his virginity on an ugly, coffee-stained blue couch his cousin sold him for fifty dollars. More exciting than the sex that continued intermittently for two hours was the authentic and fresh experience of being an accessory to adultery, which gave his life, very much in danger of becoming irrevocably unremarkable, some flavor, a touch of melodramatic meaning. That Hans fell asleep naked on the couch, in total disregard of the danger of Geoff returning home early, alone redeemed Rodney from all of his recent failures.

Just as Rodney hoped, the affair did turn out to be the antidote to the hours he found himself wasting as an office grunt. Hans and Rodney met five more times, which were never planned. Their relationship was one that neither of them bothered to define except through actions. When they talked, it was often about politics and culture and, of course, their hoped-for futures. They enjoyed indulging in each others' ambitions nearly as much as they did their bodies.

The affair lasted almost exactly two months. The end was announced when he heard Hans and Geoff arguing again, this time at 1 a.m. on a weekday and with numerous references to both his name and the "fucking piece of shit downstairs." Sensibly viewing confrontation as a waste of energy and time, Rodney started packing as the fight increased in tenor and pitch and spent the next day at a friend's apartment. He wrote a letter for Hans, a declaration of his feelings of (well, not exactly love), capped off by his cell phone number, and sneaked into the upstairs apartment when he knew that Geoff would be gone to hide his letter in Hans's gym bag. It was only a polite gesture. Rodney was neither surprised nor disappointed that he never heard from Hans again.

What Rodney did mourn was the severing of the one thread keeping his ambitions from shattering on the concrete. Hans's dreams had illuminated his own aspirations like the moon. Without him they were simply as cold and dead and pointless as an ugly, scarred rock floating in the void. Overnight even the cultural capital of the world had been scorched clean of any and all promises of victory. Only an infinite series of temp and part-time office jobs unrolled under him like all the circles of Hell.

Thus when Rodney's mother e-mailed him about a job opening at Dead End's one major newspaper, the *Weekly Observer,* he was vulnerable on every level, from the spiritual down to the financial. With hardly any ceremony, he said goodbye to his couple of New York friends and took a train down to Dead End and a future as empty as the Gobi and just as seemingly infinite.

2

For the convenience of the reader, the following is a succinct timeline of Rodney Bauman's history at Dead End for the first two years he worked at the *Weekly Observer:*

One month, two weeks, and five days—Rodney still believed that the job would only be temporary and that at any time some publication in DC, New York, Boston, San Francisco, Los Angeles, Seattle, or London would be magnanimous enough to summon him for an interview.

Two months and one day—He realized that he was so anxious to hear from possible employers he was checking his e-mail approximately thirteen to twenty-seven times an afternoon. This realization did not alter his habits in the slightest.

Four months, four weeks, and one day— Finally he finished unpacking and put a perfect minimum of effort into putting his own personality and tastes up on display in his townhouse (three movie posters, one family picture, two couches, a cheap, secondhand dining room set, and an unremarkable and mismatched chair he chose himself.)

Six months—The effort Rodney directed toward job hunting had been steadily decreasing since roughly the three month mark, but by now it had went down by approximately three-fourths.

Nine months—Gradually he realized with existential horror that he had established a routine as inflexible as that experienced by any prisoner or school student: Sundays were the days designated for tending to laundry and grocery shopping, Thursdays were for renting movies—but never more than two, and Fridays were-excellent-margaritas-and-mediocre-taco salads at the local Mexican restaurant with one of his few friends from childhood who had stayed in town.

One year—Astonishingly the thought that he had lived and worked in Dead End for one year did not occur to him.

One year and two months and four days—For about twenty-three minutes he thought idly about killing himself. He was dissuaded from that course of action solely by the realization that he did not want his sole contribution to world history to be ruining an EMT's night.

Nearly two years—Rodney had still not escaped.

Boiled down to its substantive components and measured quantitatively, Rodney's job as staff writer for the *Weekly Observer* was 3% answering phone calls from the tediously deranged, 45% condensing information from government bodies and various prominent organizations in order to be processed by the less than 20% of local citizens who even bothered,

30% either scouring the Internet for opportunities he had no gall to seek out in the flesh or trying to entertain himself by studiously learning about all the local adulteries and corruptions and other bits of real news that could never go into the paper, and 2% conducting interviews with local officials he had a duty to please and self-declared Concerned Citizens (the capitalizations were implied every single time) who found the meaning of life buried deep in the trivial.

Only a week into the job he decided that his boss and editor-in-chief Lucinda was a fellow inmate. The immediate clue was the way she decorated her office. Not a single framed article decorated the retro wood-panel walls. No plastic trophy, bestowed on her for her service to the community, was in evidence. The only flourishes were three art deco prints haphazardly placed on one of the walls. Perhaps the only other decoration worth noting was how the yellowed and dust-caked Venetian blinds always kept the room thick with darkness in militant defiance of the brightest days, making the perfect accompaniment to the perpetual stench of cigarette smoke.

Lucinda, who subconsciously made herself look like a big city editor with aggressively fashionable clothing and a neo-aristocratic air, somehow managed to simultaneously live for and disdain the perks of being part of a small city's elite. She remonstrated with Rodney even as she ordered him to write stories about such topics as the never ending plague of mold in the high school building and the opening of an antique toy car museum in a retired bus driver's basement. It was especially her stories about Rev. Lou Meredith, and how he presided over the city like a sanctified Al Capote or an emperor-televanglist, that helped sustain Rodney and his fragile spirit from week to week.

Despite his position in the community, Rodney suspected that the Rev. Meredith would remain a distant reality, one that would lurk in casual conversation and overshadow some of his stories but never would manifest himself. Then, miraculously, one day Rev. Meredith appeared as if summoned in Rodney's cramped, featureless office. As if on a melodramatic cue, it had started raining outside with thick drops that battered the tiny, high, cobweb-choked window that was Rodney's only visual outlet to the outside world. The Reverend was a very tall man who spent his life aspiring toward a presence that was paradoxically regal and folksy but only accomplished carving out a natural expression that was merely warmly authoritarian, like a small town therapist or a school principal striving to actually be popular with both faculty and students. His frail frame contrasted unpleasantly with a jutting gut, which could have either been an ambitious tumor or a blasphemous pregnancy. That day, the day His Eminence chose to reveal himself to Rodney, he was wearing a blue navy suit with a red-and-black tie as if the outfit was a second skin, the sort of trick only a true, God-chosen member of the American nobility can pull off.

Seeing a man in his office he had only known through the magic of television and who had his name written across the nation many, many times over the past few decades awakened a stirring within Rodney that had been more or less dormant for nearly a year. During the general introductions and the handshake, Rodney, as much as Meredith's preferred political cocktail of modernized theocracy and survival-of-the-fittest capitalism made him feel slightly uneasy, in much the same way the mouse would be discomforted by having a cordial meeting with the owl, was elated to be shaking hands with someone that was simply *known*.

"Mr. Bauman, it is a pleasure to finally meet you," Meredith said in a voice that magically conveyed right away a personal, sincere interest in the other's needs and wants. "I read your series on the Roosevelt Street bed and breakfast renovation with interest."

"Oh, thank you. It was really nothing, though."

As Rodney would have expected, Meredith got down to business the nanosecond he was sure that the requisite number of pleasantries had been paid.

"Last week a member of my congregation came to me regarding a reading assignment given to her daughter, Melody Harrow." With that, his smile became disturbingly broad. "She was, ah, distraught because the reading material assigned to Melody was clearly inappropriate and inflammatory. It was..." Meredith hesitated, as if he did not want to give the book the honor of casually remembering it. "... yes, it was *Suddenly, Last Summer,* a play."

"The Tennessee Williams play?"

"Yes, I believe so. Mrs. Harrow feels, and I am in total agreement, that the play is totally unsuitable for... well, especially for a young girl of Melody's impressionable age." With a flair passed down by generations of Protestants, Meredith slipped just a little into his preacher persona. "She said that Melody was in tears that day she came home, horrified that she was forced to read a play about a homosexual who exploits his young cousin to attract... *lovers.*" Saint Paul would have envied Meredith's capacity for soul-deep revulsion. However, Rodney only had a slight glimpse of negative feeling, one that was quickly submerged beneath Meredith's aura of avuncular benevolence.

Whatever his own political sympathies,

Rodney's instincts made his heart change pace and switched his mind into another level of awareness. Here was a chance, one that may as well have been delivered by angels emerging from the bowels of the Arc of the Covenant, to be at ground zero of Rev. Meredith's newest media gaffe. Hopefully, it would be one on the same scope and scale as the time he declared on national television that the Vietnam War was God's punishment for the Sexual Revolution.

If Meredith made a similar pronouncement, Rodney would have power, if only a sliver of it, as the initial emissary to the world. It would be an event that would perhaps give Rodney a month, a week, ten minutes within the pearly gates of fame. Lord, Lord, Rodney would have prayed if years of witnessing his peers pray for their chosen teams to win Super Bowls or pass American History tests hadn't paradoxically convinced him of the uselessness of prayer, let this be it, let me at least have a taste of what I crave, a crack through the walls surrounding Eden to peer through.

Without realizing it Rodney leaned forward. For the first time in his journalism career, he felt engaged in an interview.

"And what grade level is Melody?" Rodney fought to keep down his unexpected surge of enthusiasm.

"A senior in high school. Next year she will be attending Patriot University on a full scholarship." Somehow Meredith had made that sentence sound like a sales pitch, an advertisement as crass as any TV commercial for children's sugary cereal.

"Can you say more about how she felt about the book?"

"She was appalled. She had been homeschooled until the ninth grade, so she as well as her mother were unprepared for what passes for literature in the secular world." Rodney was pleased that Meredith felt secure in speaking the private, sacred language he reserved when addressing the perpetually optimistic young people at Patriot University or the hatted old ladies in 1976's fashions among his congregation. Did Meredith see him not as a potential foe, out to extract a pound of flesh for the grand secularist conspiracy, or even as a Gentile, but as a fellow believer?

Unfortunately, like any person who cultivated their fame rather than stumbled across it, Meredith was a seasoned actor whose self was impossible to extricate from the role, even for him. It was something Rodney himself would have to learn, and he was an aspiring student. "What was it about the play that Melody objected to?"

"References to cannibalism and homosexuality. Now I don't want to say that there shouldn't be such... controversial topics in literature..." Rodney's hope sank down his throat, nearly choking him. Meredith was acting as if he were in potentially hostile territory after all. "... But is it really appropriate for a young girl to have to read about that? Melody and her mother were especially concerned that Sebastian's mother is portrayed as outright evil, even though she is simply the concerned mother of a homosexual son whose life ended in agony and disgrace."

Despite Meredith not being as open as Rodney would have liked, it required only a little prompting from Rodney for Meredith to outline his plan of action for dealing with Mr. McKenzie, the teacher who falsely anticipated that his seventeen and eighteen-year old students would be able to handle adult fiction. At the next school board meeting, both Meredith and Melody's concerned parents would make a dramatic appearance, demanding Mr. McKenzie's dismissal. If their demands were not meant, then they would, in Meredith's phrase, "pile on the pressure" until at last the tumor was removed from the local educational system.

"We will go to the state educational board, if it is necessary," Meredith said, his gentle smile at odds with the implications of his words.

"And did Melody actually read the entire play?"

"She read enough of it. Fortunately her parents were able to convince Mr. McKenzie to accept some alternate reading, the play *Our Town*."

"Even though he was flexible, you still think he should be dismissed? I mean..." Rodney hesitated, wondering if it was risky to extend such bait for a predator as large and as dangerous as the Rev. Meredith. "This is a person's livelihood."

Rodney hoped that Meredith would rail some more against the teacher who dared assume his adult student had adult sensibilities, but Meredith merely wore the casual demeanor of a time-lost encyclopedia salesman.

"I realize it's... it's a bit aggressive, but I do think Mr. McKenzie was deliberately trying to make a point, to maybe fire a shot in the culture war."

"Culture war?" Rodney accidentally verbalized his thoughts. The phrase was one that previously danced only on the periphery of his awareness of national events, but immediately he enjoyed the phrase's flavor.

"Yes. An attack on the values of the American Christian majority." Clearly the words and their precise order had been repeated many, many times. "It is an attempt to impose the values of... certain segments of the population."

"That's a lot to put on a high school teacher." Rodney was now only flailing at Meredith's diplomatic armor.

"Well, we have found after only a little research that Mr. McKenzie has pushed controversial subject matter on his students before and has been reprimanded in the past. Like when he taught a play from the Renaissance about a man who sells his soul to Satan."

"*Faust*?"

"Oh, yes, forgive me." Meredith chuckled. "Not good reading for an impressionable student. And from what I understand that play is also written by a homosexual."

That evening, Rodney nursed his disappointment over the interview with an all but tasteless microwaved spaghetti dinner and the finest wine that could be picked up from a discount grocery store. Absolutely nothing Meredith said or even implied couldn't be found already on any given right-wing newspaper column or Internet screed. Sure, the idea of a vengeful media deity targeting a powerless American teacher could offer some controversy, but there was no junk food there to entice the media. Rodney had been bled dry of patriotic sentiment by sociocultural forces he could barely explain and, like most self-conscious journalists today, he had no feeling for John Q. Public except a vague dismissive contempt far from either love or hate. Still, Rodney knew as well as any sociological scholar what the American public not only wanted, but needed. The tragedy was that, unless Meredith offered him a crumb, he would have to wait for something along the lines of some morbid murder or kidnapping involving a pretty, media-friendly white child or woman.

As Rodney ate, he checked his e-mail for the sixteenth time that day (nothing except a political forward from an uncle that linked abortion to gay marriage in a novel and somewhat unexpected way). In the past he had hope—small, murky, undefined, but still hope—that something unpredictable would come along, even if only in the form of one solitary e-mail. This was the first day he could remember since he had returned to Dead End that he had no hope whatsoever. Suddenly before Rodney came a dark vision, a calendar built of blank white cells filled with being trapped in a desolate small city, with school board meetings revolving around hours-long debates about the budget. It would be a life where the only remaining truly important event would be death. Perhaps, Rodney wondered with another serving of bland, heavily processed pasta around his spoon, that was all he deserved. Perhaps his ambition was placed within him accidentally, a fluke or a deliberate act of cosmic cruelty.

"Why do you doubt?" A deep unexpected voice said, shocking Rodney so badly that he leaped up from his chair and dropped his sauce-dipped spoon to the floor.

Standing across from his kitchen/dining room/ living room table was Jesus—not as Americans would wish him to be, with a square jaw worthy of Superman, a well-trimmed beard gold like rows of wheat, and skin that would not be misplaced on a Scandinavian. No, instead it was Jesus as He most likely was, just dark enough he would have been harassed in the Deep South and a beard in desperate need of a pair of scissors. Certainly he was not nearly as handsome as Willem DeFoe or Christian Bale in their prime. There was no divine light glowing from his body, no long lavish robes flowing like a holy river, only a plain and occasionally stained mantle covering a tunic.

Rodney's meager and slipshod religious training had not even begun to prepare him for this momentous occasion, desired by millions but unexpected and unwanted by him. A part of his mind urged him to kneel and slobber exaltations to the floor, but instead these words escaped from his mouth: "Why are you here?"

Jesus did not respond, not with words at any rate, but instead engaged Rodney's eyes with his own. His stare was stern and intimate. Jesus spoke again. "Why have you allowed your heart to become hardened?"

At that, Rodney did fall to his knees. Jesus touched him lightly on the shoulder. The voice softened, but remained authoritative. It was the voice of a therapist, a teacher, and a police officer in one. "You have been gifted with a passion, and yet you believe that it will be squandered. No, there is one who will inspire you, and you shall go into the world and find what you have sought."

With that, the holy presence vanished completely, and Rodney was left with a half-finished dinner and a tiny stain on the carpet.

Rodney did not allow himself the luxury of wondering if he had gone catastrophically insane. At any rate, who could afford to have a total psychotic break these days? Instead he cleaned the stain, finished his dinner, and went about the evening as he usually did. What else could he do?

3

Although Rodney was in a state of absolute denial about his unwanted religious revelation, he did have a sense of revitalization that was growing deep in the core of his mind. Perhaps the appearance of a Jewish philosopher and alleged son of God in his living room had been a none too subtle sign from a higher power, a divine broadcast from fate, or a spectacular delusion bubbling out of the Jungian collective unconscious. No more was he simply the conveyor of trial verdicts and school year statistics and high school sports scores. Now he was a storyteller for the masses, an advocate for the powerless, linking readers from their sofas and kitchen tables and desks to a fight that spanned the cultural, political, social, and religious landscapes and, better yet, opened up a smoking front in their backyards. The Great Tennessee Williams Scandal of Dead End could be his salvation after all.

In his mind Rodney perfected every single detail of what had to, what must unfold. Already he had written and published his article on the showdown between a forsaken public servant and the forces of perpetual uptightness. Mr. McKenzie, a small red-headed man who still looked as if his freshman year of college was just a year behind him, was fixed firmly against the barbarian army of scolds rallied against him in the meeting room of the school board, sated on day-old coffee and pastries.

McKenzie had been deprived from birth of the raw glamor mandated for even a halfway-decent martyr. By any reasonable standard, McKenzie was nothing to take a second glance at, a genuine lifeless ordinary, but Rodney did not have to think long before he decided that McKenzie was the ideal primordial clay, who would be molded into more through the magic of journalism.

Instead of appearing mortified when he stepped forward before the five members of the school board and the superintendent to deliver his defense of himself, educational standards, and Tennessee Williams, Rodney would have him stand before the tanks of the opposition like he knew he was in the service of history. The flaccid apology McKenzie offered up to the callous crowd, "Although we disagree, I am sorry for the distress this whole situation has been causing," was erased totally from the record. In his article McKenzie did not have half a damn to spare for any Philistines who were convinced that a seventeen year old high school student, if not all of American society, is too brittle for Tennessee Williams. Even if he was not at all up to it in the flesh, on paper McKenzie would become a champion of the right of youth to be allowed passage into the real world.

When the school board decided to come to a decision on the matter in two weeks, Rodney was forced to repress a cheer. There would be no smothering this controversy in its crib, at least not if he could stand vigilant. At the end of the meeting, when most people, especially the board members, scurried off, Rodney asked McKenzie whether or not he expected Melody's defenders to drag this out.

"Well, I... I definitely hope not. The sooner we can put it all behind us the better, as far as I am concerned."

Rodney silently wished he had a more reckless hero for this struggle. "But if they do continue this? What then?" Deciding for a second to forgo patience, Rodney also threw in, "Will you put up a fight?"

The mere appearance of a word like "fight" startled McKenzie like a gunshot. "I don't know," he replied with instinctual cowardice. "I suppose I'll have to, if my job is at stake."

"Do you think there's more at stake than that?"

"Oh! Well, yeah, I guess there is. It would be a shame to have a precedent that says seniors in high school can't handle hearing swear words and learning that not everyone just gets a job and gets married and has kids." That was enough for now.

The first barrier, a mark of official approval from Lucinda, was bypassed without any strain. Eager to leave the office behind as she was every Friday, Lucinda gave the article the highest words of approval that Rodney ever heard from her on any matter involving the newspaper.

"It's fine," she said.

"Okay," he said, matching her apathy for apathy. With practiced casualness, he added, "What about a series?"

"Just on this teacher?"

"No, no. Well, not really. I mean, if this whole thing actually builds up, we can follow it, right? Step by step?"

As Rodney predicted, Lucinda gave a shrug and spoke as she made it for the door, "Whatever will fill column inches."

For the first time Rodney could look at that week's edition with satisfaction. The article in black and white, with a picture of McKenzie standing stoically with a well-worn 1982 edition of *Suddenly, Last Summer,* symbolized the successful unfolding of phase one. The next phase would involve carefully following, with hopefully four or five articles, the controversy, from the cost being paid by McKenzie to Rev. Meredith's battle strategy against McKenzie and the whole educational system to what side the public leans toward. Then, finally, there would be the last article, detailing a victory and a defeat, where Rodney would dare drag a small city newspaper out of its usual cozy home and force it to carry questions on censorship and culture and education. In the end, his series will be seen as a poignant gaze on a teacher brought to task for failing to win the entire community's approval before he handed out a simple reading assignment. It would make a perfectly respectable foundation of the portfolio he could present to a major newspaper. Or perhaps, just as well, he would be mentioned in biographies of the Rev. Meredith as the reporter who stood up against him for the sake of defending the principles of a lone high school teacher.

Exactly one week and one day before the decisive school board meeting Rodney received an unanticipated call from McKenzie. From the very start of the mandatory pleasantries McKenzie sounded relieved and almost vindicated.

"I resigned," he finally said. "I kind of thought you should know. By this summer I'll be gone."

Rodney's posture and expressions was those of a puppeteer who had unexpectedly found that his strings had been cruelly sabotaged.

"My sister-in-law is good friends with an administrator who works for this private school in Massachusetts," he explained without prompting. "They officially offered me a job and it seems like a good place."

"What about– I mean, weren't you willing to fight this?" The tone of Rodney's voice was nearly the exact equivalent of a disappointed teenager at the precise moment they find out that the star athlete they idolize was found guilty of murdering a child prostitute in a heroin-induced rage.

"It wasn't just the whole... situation that prompted my decision, really. Besides... well, can I say something off the record, please?"

Rodney surprised himself by not lying. "Yeah, sure."

"If there is a fight—I mean, like, politically—I think in a place like here it was lost decades ago, you know?"

"Yeah, maybe." In his mind Rodney wished his one-time hero the very worst.

So the only other story Rodney wrote about the Great Tennessee Williams Scandal was a dry account of Mr. McKenzie leaving Dead End City Schools for good. It was pure paint-by-numbers, with shining quotes from students and the principal, and McKenzie elaborating on his plans for his future and describing his time in Dead End with words that were not from any angle truthful. The number of words Rodney spent mentioning the Great Tennessee Williams Scandal were exactly twelve in the first draft and cut down to seven in the second.

"That's it for a series then?" Lucinda asked as another day preparing for press in the office wound down. As always she was smoking a cigarette in the office to celebrate the happy occasion, as much for pure physical pleasure as for the intangible joy of defying the anti-smoking decrees of both the corporate office and society at large.

"Yeah. And I had all this research on censorship in high schools prepared too. It would have been interesting. Well, if I can say so."

"Especially since they would have gotten that guy's ass in a sling," Lucinda said in what was no doubt a perfect prophecy.

"Right," Rodney said. On impulse Rodney asked suddenly, "Do you like working here? I mean, you don't mind being here?"

Lucinda crushed her cigarette in the ash tray,

strategically placed in the middle of the drafting room. "I don't know. I'm not all that unhappy, I have a decent enough social life although I can't hold down a boyfriend if my life depended on it, I'm not living paycheck to paycheck, and I get to strut around this goddamn town like some kind of bigshot."

She sighed and waved her hands as though making a secret signal. "It could be worse, you know, Rod. Everything can always be worse."

As they walked out of the office, Rodney could not refrain from asking one more question. "What do you want to be when you grow up?"

Lucinda laughed, even though she must have caught the faint sound of the seemingly misplaced gravitas in Rodney's voice.

"A senator." She took a few steps toward her car and then twirled around to add, "At the very least."

The next day, a scorching June Saturday, Rodney once again pushed into his mental trash heap thoughts of achieving anything beyond the usual anorexic paycheck and decided to squander the day on searching for a new after-work refuge. His old choice, a coffee joint in downtown Dead End, had been a place for having an excuse not to return home since high school, but since he moved back it had gone out with hardly a whimper like so many other Dead End small businesses.

The city council had for years promised that they would "revitalize" downtown. Rodney knew this better than anyone, since he had to write an article on "downtown revitalization" at an average of every four months. Their efforts had mainly resulted in a few new antique stores here and there in a downtown that already swarmed with them, a theater where more than half the shows were local high school and college productions, and a market where the most unique and exotic offering was a Japanese steak house. Towering over these small steps toward an economic resurrection were the same strung-up corpses of stores and businesses long dead.

He could not remember the last time he had truly roamed around the downtown area. Faintly he hoped he might stumble across someplace new, some fresh gap in the monotony. The only promising lifeline he could find was a new venue, a coffee shop/ bookstore hybrid that proudly bore the unambitious name *The Shire* with the agonizingly quaint image of a hobbit-esque entity reclining in a blue lounge chair and smoking circles into being with a pipe. The interior could only be described as looking like a coffee shop and deli dropped in the middle of a medium-sized bookstore, although the concept was to Rodney's liking. Good coffee and book businesses were among the many luxuries of twenty-first life that were severely lacking in Dead End.

Deciding he might as well take lunch here, Rodney ordered a tuna sandwich with fries and a soda, his customary way to christen a new eatery. He could not help but notice the cook, a tall man with a tight but well-proportioned face and revealing slight symptoms of a swimmer's build even under an ugly green apron more than slightly too big for him. His hair was long and light brown; it was ineptly hidden under a baseball cap, but such shoddy concealment only encouraged Rodney's nascent yet already strong attraction.

Of course, Rodney did not need the benefit of experience to know that flirting with men openly in a place like Dead End was an invitation for humiliation at the very best. So to distract himself from the cook's allure Rodney browsed the shelves. After surveying the poor selections in history and literature, he discovered that all the books in the religious section were about Christianity—mostly American Protestant Christianity, at that—and the majority of works in the political section all urged the reader to be weary of how their way of life was being endangered by some group that to the untrained eye seemed disadvantaged. In short, Rodney realized this was not the best place for a young, homosexual man to practice any mating rituals.

With the logic of the helplessly outgunned, Rodney decided that, if he was deep in enemy territory, he may as well offend their sensibilities. So he sat himself down at the table nearest to the small grill where the cook labored and watched. Only once did the cook deign to return his objectifying gaze, and Rodney could not tell if it was a glance of concentrated apathy or outright disdain. When his food was served, Rodney was caught between hoping that the cook did not spit in his tuna and wishing that the cook had slipped his number somewhere between his fries.

At the same time, Rodney knew that the uncertainty was a foundational part of the appeal. An obvious return on his admiration could only break the strange magic of the situation. Indeed, any overt show of emotion would force the spell to its limits. His balanced features were emotionally sterilized, his small lips were clinched shut. As he ate Rodney began to fantasize that he had found his perfect nemesis, someone who could not be bothered to give half a damn about ambition or his job or even his station in life, and faced every twist and turn with the same cool, black-booted expression.

Would Rev. Meredith call this culture war, Rodney asked himself? Studying a cook in a religiously-themed bookstore and café, positioning him in fantasy worlds as elaborate as anything in J.R.R. Tolkien, and lusting after him with an intensity Rodney had not even felt since he was first pulled into the gravitational pull of Dead End. Perhaps this alone enlisted him into the front lines, his libido and an imagination that can only come from a lifetime of sexual frustration his only weapons.

The waitress/clerk, who did not seem to share Rodney's fascination, asked the cook if there was any mayonnaise at hand. Without responding, either with a word or a nod, the cook left his post for a back room, from where he shortly returned with the sought-after mayonnaise jar. Silently he handed her the jar and turned back to the post, as if the most basic of interactions with his co-worker was beneath him. At a glimpse, she looked slightly exasperated but not surprised by the cook's stoniness. His effortless indifference, which seemed elaborately constructed as a ward against casual pleasantries, only convinced Rodney that he had found a work of art created only for him.

Sooner or later all exhibitions have to close, and Rodney was willing to just leave his tip and go home and take the time to gather together and savor all the fantasies he sketched around the enigmatic cook before they evaporated. To his surprise, the cook held Rodney hostage with a focused stare and performed a quick, sharp nod to deal the killing stroke. Even though Rodney was actually too shocked by the unexpected intrusion of fantasy into reality to say anything, the cook then made a gesture toward the back area of the store, a movement that might have been too quick to be noticed if lust had not carried off Rodney to a primal, instinctual state where all his senses were heightened.

"I'm taking my break. Right now," he said, in a tone guaranteed to destroy objections.

Rodney followed, aware that he may be walking his way into becoming the object of some old-fashioned bigoted violence, in which case he wondered if he would be entitled to write his own news article. On the bright side, even that would be a welcome change of pace.

Without even a glance back, the cook led him through the Politics and Poetry sections into a small bluish-green and otherwise featureless room that had found employment as a storage room for books. Orderly shelves lined both walls, making an already smothering room even more oppressive.

Rodney shuddered as the cook brushed his arm against him to close the door. "I saw you looking," the cook said, just several seconds before kissing him.

Without much of a preamble, the cook had Rodney against the bookshelf, hissing to himself as Rodney tried to squash any noise. It was carried out with all the pragmatism of a truly unlawful act: with as little disturbance as possible and a minimum of clothing being let loose. Rodney even made the effort not to hit his face against the shelves, although his hands, searching for a grip, accidentally knocked loose two books. The first somersaulted straight down to the wood floor and exposed the title *The Myth of Homosexual AIDS* and the second made a crash landing against Rodney's knee and landed on its back with its front blaring the words, *God's Grace and the Homosexual Next Door.* Understandably Rodney was too distracted to appreciate the coincidence at the height of the moment, but he still had the presence of mind to realize with some satisfaction that this was sex without the purpose of love or pleasure, without even the primitive purpose of satisfying the itch to fuck. It was sex as a spontaneous act of secret defiance, of letting loose psychic contamination.

Once both cook and customer were satisfied, the cook merely smoothed out his clothes, gave Rodney half a nod, and cautiously opened the door, as if in the midst of a daring escape. As Rodney stood just outside the storage room, his mind refusing to fully process recent events, the cook said without facing him, "This Wednesday my shift ends at 7. I want you to meet me."

"Okay" was the best Rodney could manage.

As the cook without a word began to make his way back to his station, tying his apron behind him on the way, Rodney spit out, "What's your name?"

"S-Y-D," he replied, not stopping for a second.

4

Every generation there are only a few people like Rodney who are lucky enough to have their own personal vision on the road to Damascus. Even fewer actually deserve one. And almost no one is allotted two in one lifetime. However, Rodney was a uniquely blessed mediocrity, something he himself was beginning to realize because of the afternoon at *The Shire*, which was a revelation worthy of a dozen stumbling adolescent fantasies and which was an even clearer sign from above than the impromptu visit by Jesus Christ. The experience of Syd had cracked open the shell of lethargy that had gradually grown, mold-like, around Rodney all these years. After all it was perhaps a miracle that could lead to other miracles, and what could be more miraculous than unprotected sex with a perfect stranger in the storeroom of a

Christian book store?

His mind humming and churning, Rodney, over a plate of lukewarm Rice-a-Roni, connected all the signs he had been given, from Rev. Meredith's words and straight across to the books that were revealed to him like occult messages during his time with Syd. All lines headed back to the words "Culture War," which had been washed clean of its absurdities, revealing underneath a fresh profoundness, a coded command, that Rodney could not possibly ignore, even if he had the inclination. By virtue of simply being a gay man Rodney was already enlisted and trained and armed as a front-line soldier in the Culture War, making enclaves in the suburbs and the small towns, planting ideas that incinerate housewives and Eagle Scouts, leaving in the ashes serial monogamists and bisexual, genderqueer Philosophy majors.

Culture War. Rodney could barely sleep that night because he was illuminated with the knowledge that this had to be his *raison d'etre*; the only genuine question was whether or not he was born to write on the Culture War or if the idea of Cultural War was carefully, delicately poured into someone's mind just for him. He would take this little concept and turn it into a job for a high-profile newspaper, two or three bestselling books, a nice house somewhere in the suburbs of New York City or Boston, and his name being written down and talked about at least a hundred times a day across the nation. True, it was nothing but a meaningless phrase from the mouths of brainless talking heads, yet it was also a precious seed Rodney was meant to care for and that would grow into the *deus ex machina* that would change his story for the better.

But how to take the first step? The next day

at the newspaper Rodney searched for anything that could be used as grist for the inaugural article on the Culture War, but he knew once he dipped his foot in the water that the people of Dead End would be distressingly uncooperative. The most he could dig up through the newspaper's own files was a local gang who were disappointingly unenterprising in their occasional incursions into the classic art of vandalism and were clearly motivated by nothing more profound than white bourgeois boredom. There were no gay bars and the closest thing to radical groups in Dead End were safely confined to the local secular colleges, Rivermont University and Spencer College. (Unfortunately, no one ever thought it appropriate to have a "Dead End College.") Rodney only learned that for the past five years every potential, promising controversy in the area had been snuffed out with Mafia efficiency. It seemed Culture War was breaking out almost everywhere in the country, but Dead End was already occupied territory.

Rodney understood patience—not as a virtue, of course, but as a necessity. He was very much aware of time pressing down on him, a suffocating pillow that did its work with geological slowness, and hunted for any scrap of a story that would welcome his angle. For two and a half weeks he waited, and when he read a notice that a postmodern art exhibit would come to town his heart jumped. Visions of cherished religious symbols cheerfully immersed in bodily fluids, George W. Bush juxtaposed with Pol Pot, and a loop of video footage showing actors wearing masks modeled after prominent Republican senators masturbating to Holocaust footage danced merrily in his head.

When Rodney arrived at the exhibit with his camera and a notepad in tow, he had to fight the urge to skip into the university hall. Sadly, the actual exhibit, which filled only two galleries, failed utterly to meet his lofty expectations. Rodney came starving for controversy, and instead he found only artifacts that barely had the power to shock the most sheltered and uptight of suburbanites. In one room there were the usual Jackson Pollack-esque abstracts that invoked thoughts of nothing except hideous motel wallpaper, bland replications of scenes from a soap opera from an artist who felt free to declare that he had nothing but contempt for his own source of "inspiration," and a large recreation of the artist's kitchen, down to a profoundly filthy coffee pot and a surprisingly uninspired upper middle-class dinner set.

Staggered by disappointment, Rodney somehow made his way into the second gallery, where some tiny sliver of hope beckoned. The centerpiece of this gallery was work by the only avant-garde artist Rodney knew by name and reputation, an unknown and politically motivated left-wing vandal known only as "Zmora" whose cultivated notoriety and presumed urban authenticity delighted his rich, overeducated patrons and in turn injected them with a sense of rough-edged intellectual vitality as potent as it was unjustified. Perhaps the vandal's one truly great artistic accomplishment was making his handlers look like so many adolescents trapped in cushy, bright neighborhoods not even within a bus line's reach of the ghetto, seizing desperately upon anything that spoke of Friday night gunfire and casual, unrubbered sex. Sadly, Rodney felt none of those thrills as he gazed upon a mannequin dressed as a cop in riding gear riding on a toy horse, fish fingers in an aquarium, and a painting of an eighteenth century aristocratic woman with a Groucho Marx mask glued to it. If he was supposed to be standing right at the cutting edge, Rodney shuddered to think at what the proud gatekeepers of the modern art world would dismiss as passe.

Now filled with despair at the sight of another route being closed shut before him, Rodney turned to the person placed in charge of the exhibit, Professor Morrison, a tall man in his late thirties who in his dress and mannerisms far more resembled an accountant entrenched totally in some corporate microcosm than a specialist in postmodern anything, and asked him a question for his readers that he hoped would prove a tempting opening for a good enraging statement or two.

"So, let's start with the obvious question. What is art?" he asked.

"Whatever the hell people with money say it is," he answered with no hesitation and absolute sincerity. Rodney looked for provocation in the rest of the interview, but continued running against an academically perfected apathy. The least Rodney hoped to wring from Professor Morrison was a blithe dismissal of the plebian atmosphere of places like Dead End. Instead Morrison, with all the enthusiasm of a hungover fast food cashier, concluded the interview by inviting the plebs to challenge their preconceptions. Rodney was disappointed but in the overview not at all surprised that contemporary art had failed him so spectacularly.

There were only two real pleasures that sustained him through this terrible new era of anticipation. The first were margaritas at his preferred Mexican restaurant and the second was Syd, whose rendezvous with him began to take place on a roughly weekly basis. For their next meeting they managed to sneak into one of the dorms in Patriot University, where, Syd casually informed him, he had dropped out a few years ago. Syd talked his way into his old dorm building, claiming that he was on campus for an alumni event and wanted to tour his old haunts with his friend, and selected a particularly hot, cramped study room. The tightness of the space, the grinding discomfort, and the odd Lovecraftian geometric angles imposed on his body, only heightened and perfected the experience of the sex, as did the strong possibility of horrifying an unlucky innocent bystander, if any student who would want to use a dorm study room for official, legitimate purposes ever actually existed in the entire history of universities.

The week after Syd chose a location and chose midnight in front of the statue of a Confederate lieutenant, someone who lost half an arm and then an ear saving Dead End from Yankees mad on gunpowder and nationalism. This time Syd delayed gratification to fondle and caress Rodney's body before he took him with Rodney's head resting against the cold stone of the soldier's boot. From behind the oak trees surrounding the statue a middle-aged homeless man with a face almost artistically decorated with wrinkles and scars was watching and he hissed what sounded like "fags" as he blatantly masturbated, mumbling broken phrases to himself with every successful stroke. It was a chorus sung for the benefit of a man who lost two appendages in the name of a sterile and doomed government.

As Rodney walked awkwardly, cautiously with Syd back to their cars, simultaneously frightened and thrilled that their one-man audience might be following him and on the verge of turning violent, he struggled to devise a strategy that would force Syd to say something more than simply when they would meet to fuck again.

"So, is there a point to all this?" Rodney asked. Instantly he was embarrassed by his accidental attempt to inject significance into the relationship.

Syd stopped and looked toward the pavement, as if entering a state of profound contemplation. "A point? We fucked. That's a point."

"I know, and I... I enjoy seeing you, or... whatever you want to call this. But I have to ask is this leading to something... else?"

"You mean a relationship? Phone calls, dates, moving in? That shit?"

Rodney shuddered.

"Something kind of like that, I... I think."

Syd laughed, the first time Rodney had ever been privy to the sound. It was not entirely pleasant or unpleasant.

"We already got a relationship."

Of course, Rodney did not want to end it, whatever *it* was. In fact, he knew that he could not end it. He had wondered if he had fallen in love, but it wasn't the love from the films and from gushing newly engaged couples that came from some sort of abstract completion. Instead it was a love that came from a scratched itch, a need and its fulfillment, some desire that had roots that ran deep down into the psychological plane, perhaps even breaking into the mystical. It was much more than sex, Rodney knew, and he believed Syd knew too.

"We do" was all Rodney could say. Syd expressed a sharp nod.

"What we've got is our own. It's enough."

Rodney agreed.

"This Friday, I want you to meet me back at the store, right at closing time at 10 p.m. There's some other places there that I want us to consecrate."

Rodney felt relief pulse through him. "I'll see you there."

His mind aflame, Rodney could not really sleep that night, but was instead stranded at the furthest borders of consciousness with nonsense thoughts and half-digested memories. Suddenly, cutting through this fog, there was a vision that was somehow neither dream nor reality. Rodney simultaneously saw and felt himself standing in what might very well have been Death Valley. He would have been perfectly alone if not for various mannequins dressed in a wide assortment of everyday and formal dresses frozen in various stages of entrapment in the ground, their free arms (and the occasional leg) artfully expressing panic like the victims of a nuclear blast stuck in their last frenzied second.

Although none of the mannequins had eyes or noses or ears, Rodney was quickly overwhelmed with a blizzard of solemn voices, the emotions they once carried decayed into a ragged monotone. It was impossible for Rodney to even begin to sift through the white noise, but there were snippets he could make out:

WANTEDTOBEAFILMMAKERWENTTOSCHOOL
GOTAJOBDOINGCOMMERCIALSMADEAMOVIE
NOBODYCARED

SHOULDHAVEGOTTENAJOBTEACHING
VICTORIANLITCOULDNTEVENGETINTOGRAD
SCHOOL

SOBADWANTEDTOGOSEECHINAANDJAPAN
NEVERNEVEREVENLEFTTHEEASTCOAST

Just when Rodney thought he would lose his very self before the horde of voices, a clear, strong voice rose above the others and they dissipated like raindrops.

"Son of man, can these ambitions live?" The voice asked. Rodney could sense no feelings or expectations in the voice, which seemed to ring from deep inside his mind.

"I don't know," Rodney said, as if rehearsing a script. Unlike his first vision, he did not even have the luxury of wondering if he was going mad. He had become a self-aware film character, a Rosencrantz simply carrying out his preordained lines and waiting for the scene to end.

"Son of man, these are the remains of those who came before you. They say, 'Our dreams are dried up and our hope is gone. We are cut off.' However, you will succeed where they have failed, and arrive at the promised land." The voice had barely finished speaking when Rodney felt the environment around him flicker from view and his sense of his flesh and mind and all slipping away from... a dream? Something less than reality, or something more? Suddenly the landscape melted away, if it had ever truly been there in the first place, and Rodney was left with only a vague idea of a place and a time. Was Syd there? Whether he was or was not, Rodney felt himself become warmed by the sense of a dream fulfilled.

"You will know what to do," the voice spoke, just as Rodney opened his eyes.

5

Like the vast majority of human beings conditioned from birth by the extremely sophisticated system of rewards and punishments typically referred to as "modern Western civilization," Rodney was cowardly. However, last night's vision, which he only remembered in faint scraps, had imbued him with an idea that demanded to be acted upon and and a courage usually experienced only by sociopaths.

At 1 o'clock, when he was usually accustomed to go to lunch, he drove two hours away to a squat building by a ramp to the by-pass. At that spot, there was a store where the windows were covered in black and the walls were painted an inconspicuous shade of blue. There he purchased twelve pornographic magazines for heterosexuals, each specializing in a different fetish, from Latino/African-American interracial women to transvestite midgets to octogenarians, and one pornographic film based rather loosely on Charlton Heston's *The Ten Commandments*. Returning home, he typed up without revisions a letter that read:

Dear Uptights,

Consider this our FIRST SHOT against your CULTURE-REGIME, our DECLARATION OF REVOLT against your shock-troops encroaching on our homes and our minds and our books and our iPods. Institutions like this Uptight-factory have thrived too long without SERIOUS AND SYSTEMATIC OPPOSITION. We declare today a holiday for posterity, when people began to demand a TRULY FREE CULTURE surgically cut loose from Uptight cancer-concepts. WE WILL SUCCEED and build our utopia of lewd and liberated art on top of your discredited Uptight manifestos. Mark the day. Even you admitted that our attack would be inevitable when you declared a CULTURE WAR. But we have not come to destroy, because elimination of opposition is the only method Uptights comprehend, but to further the natural process of CULTURAL EVOLUTION AND REVOLUTION. Only YOUR PEOPLE represent STAGNATION AND DEATH; we represent RENEWAL AND LIFE.

Sincerely,

The Culture Liberation Front

Taking a few minutes to bask in his accomplishment, Rodney printed off the letter and then meticulously packed the pornography in a cardboard box. In garish black marker, written out in a demented child's scrawl, was the address of Patriot University's Office of Promotions; there would be no return address. Hands trembling but mind unrepentant, Rodney had the package shipped.

It only took an imaginary contact, allegedly entrenched deep in Patriot University's administrative bowels, to bring the sordid details of the offensive package to the unprepared public. The only aspect that caused Rodney any degree of struggle was deciding upon the article's title: "PATRIOT UNIV NOW A FRONT IN CULTURE WAR." Rodney was careful, slipping fat buzz-phrases like "Culture Terrorists" and "War of Ideas" into the text like pills in dog food. Instinctively Lucinda appreciated the beauty of what Rodney was aspiring toward and congratulated him on scare-mongering well done.

It was a simple coup, but Rodney had learned from studious observation that the central problem with modern American journalism is that the news-reading public must be relentlessly educated on what its desires, needs, wants, fears, anxieties, loves, hates, and concerns actually are. Rodney could not allow his readers to forget or be distracted, even for just one week, but eventually the lessons he tried to teach them were stretched brittle-thin. Oh, they might bemoan the sick, sorry state of the American media in the twenty-first century, but it takes elbow grease to keep even a halfway decent scandal fresh.

Still, at first the CLF was small, almost unambitious. Several Bibles were found in the pews at Lou Meredith's church with the sexually explicit parts, from a drunk Lot being raped by his daughters to all of the *Song of Solomon,* all highlighted in hot pink. Translated copies of the Marquis de Sade's *120 Days of Sodom* and *Philosophy in the Boudoir* and Masoch's *Venus in Furs* were donated to an elementary school in the CLF's name. "The works of the Divine Marquis and Mr. Masoch is a PERFECT alternative to the WHITEWASHED G-RATED propaganda forced on OUR CHILDREN! CHILDHOOD 'INNOCENCE' IS ONLY A VICTORIAN CONSTRUCTION!", the accompanying letter declared childishly yet imperiously.

Then, without warning, the CLF's tactics escalated. Their next target was a film festival planned at a Rivermont College festival hosted by the Gender Studies department. An arduous CLF agent had managed to replace one of the planned movies, *The Hours,* with a copy of *Faster, Pussycat! Kill! Kill!* Rodney was surprised when speaking with one of the festival's organizers, an English grad student named Lauren who was clearly somewhat bemused. She sheepishly admitted that they didn't stop the film until well after the Pussycats bound and gagged Linda. Less amused was a local librarian who found that an innocuous book for children on football had all of its pages cut out and replaced with the body another book that detailed Roman gladiatorial fights.

However, the courage that was instilled in him by his second vision had a short lifespan, and the knowledge of the profoundly idiotic risks he was taking monopolized his thoughts. It was certainly luck, and not any previously untapped guerrilla skills, that had saved him from being caught, humiliated, and worse. Fortunately, Rodney was not slow to realize that the technology of his time was on his side.

It began with a name: Tammy Connery. It took Rodney weeks to construct blog post by blog post and with digital footprints here and there leading to an artificial past on the Internet. Once he was satisfied that anyone might be fooled into believing that Tammy had an existence through the medium of flesh, Rodney, perhaps taking more satisfaction in his task than any creator-god ever did, made Tammy's boyfriend, Les Green. Their relationship, as Rodney spun it into existence, was a happy and unexciting one, until she found that, in a night of unexpected drunkenness, he had sex with a co-worker. A penitent Les vowed to cut ties with his co-worker and devote himself forever to Tammy, once he learned that Tammy was pregnant with his child. Drunk on rage and feminism, Tammy had the fetus aborted at a lavishly funded Planned Parenthood clinic and informed Les through a text message simply declaring that she had the abortion just to make him suffer.

The sordid tale was told in the manner of a true

twenty-first century digital epic. Rodney regretted that this work was strictly for his career and could not be sold as a groundbreaking work in a new medium of art. First he began with a series of posts on Les's blog, which were brought to the attention of two or three national pundits. It took weeks demanding more patience than Rodney ever believed he could muster and spend, but at last, beyond his expectations, a chorus of angry talking heads were singing the exact tune Rodney had composed. Rev. Meredith himself proclaimed, in a sound byte that was regurgitated endlessly in the 24/7 news cycle, that Tammy Connery alone represented the nadir of American civilization, presumably beating out lynching, the crushing of the Philippines, and the Japanese internment camps.

After the basic narrative had time to simmer, Rodney stirred in savory details. Les had purchased a simple and classic teddy bear as his first gift to the child. Tammy was a gender studies major pursuing a career in West Coast academia. Les wanted to name the baby after the grandmother who died before he could know her if it was a girl or after his cousin who died as a soldier in Iraq if it was a boy. It was widely speculated that in high school Tammy had gotten pregnant and had another abortion then. Each fresh addition set the talking heads chattering anew, diagnosing Tammy as an irredeemable psychopath and Les as the perfect specimen of the emaciated and emasculated twenty-first century American male. Rodney recorded hours upon hours of this coverage, savoring each and every minute and realizing that this was his Sistine Chapel, filled with so many diverse and discordant elements that nonetheless added to a glorious whole.

It was only with a great deal of regret that

Rodney allowed the ruse to be revealed, three days after the story first broke which Rodney calculated was just long enough before the media would become too insistent on interviewing Les and Tammy or finding a genuine photograph. The CLF contacted Rodney directly through e-mail and demanded that he publish their statement, which decreed that, "Your all-important POLITICAL NARRATIVES are our SOAP OPERAS!" In a masterstroke Rodney had at last established himself as the one and only tether between the CLF and the general public.

Once the thrill of his accomplishment faded, Rodney felt a familiar despair eroding the edges of his consciousness. He had written a series of articles on the antics of the CLF, one filled with hazy speculations on why Dead End was chosen as the CLF's base of operations and whether or not they were a serious ideological operation or if they were just a couple of high school students drugged (at least according to one psychologist Rodney interviewed) on anti-authoritarian attitudes spread by pop music and video games. Then on an otherwise mundane Wednesday, Rodney came to work and was greeted warmly by Lucinda. The *New York Times* wanted an interview with him on the CLF.

The interview went quite well. It could not have done otherwise, since Rodney had privately rehearsed for the moment in daydreams for many years. He never expected he would perform as himself, so he was not in the slightest disappointed when he played the role of the concerned public servant. He offered readers sympathy: "I can only imagine how offensive the CLF's shock tactics might be to some people." He stoked their anxieties: "I just can't say if it's one person or a group." He went on the offensive: "The actions of the CLF are extremely concerning, not least because it just might be the start of a national trend." It took hours after the interview for Rodney to understand and interpret his own emotions this way, but he felt the fear that this would be the first and final highlight, a taste of glory that could hardly be described as fleeting.

The next day at the office, Lucinda was radiant, positively saint-like. "Ha, they've been quoting your articles all over the channels," she said. "And I've been getting ten e-mails per hour."

"You don't mind?" Rodney asked.

"Hell no. It's nice to finally be at the heart of something, you know." With that, Rodney received the very rare privilege of being treated to drinks in Lucinda's office, courtesy of the vodka she kept in her desk.

Still buzzing from his triumph long after the effects of the alcohol he drank faded, Rodney was walking to his car when a tall, thin woman with chestnut hair and a nervous expression intercepted him.

"I need you to come with me."

It took only a few seconds before Rodney realized she was holding a handgun.

6

Once the woman's rusted and impossibly alive 1986 Dodge Daytona plowed unceremoniously onto a gravel road far from any place Rodney learned the name of his kidnapper: Joy. By then Rodney's animal terror had dulled into acceptance. In the past he had imagined that like in the movies people in these types of situations instantly rediscover their instincts and become ferocious action heroes in the style of 1980s

Hollywood, but at least in his own case Rodney instead became pleasantly docile. He was Louis XVI on the way to the guillotine. He asked no questions and made no demands of the unexpected forces that had engulfed him.

"I'll tell you my real name," the woman had unexpectedly announced as orange dust engulfed the car. "It's Joy. I'm not at all afraid of possible retaliation by the authorities."

"Good to meet you, Joy," Rodney said, unintentionally ironic. She responded with something between a chuckle and a sigh.

The ice broken between captive and captor, Rodney finally asked, 'Why are you doing this? I'm nothing."

"This seemed like the only shot I'd have at getting to the Culture Liberation Front," Joy said as she navigated the vehicle near the front porch of a quasi-dilapidated two-story house that looked like one time it was at the heart of a modest little farm but now overlooked a sea of green broken only by the occasional rusted ruins of farm equipment.

At that confession of her motive, Rodney could feel his innards freeze and the bile climb to his throat. Even the cops weren't taking the CLF all that seriously, at least according to Rodney's interviews, and most people treated them like a strange nuisance that required some output of outrage but nothing more. Now there was this woman willing to commit a felony just to have a small chance at contacting the organization. He did not want to even attempt to predict what would happen if she was told she had just committed a crime for the sake of a ruse.

"Look, I don't even know how to get to them. They just contact me and they use a different e-mail address every time," he tried to explain. This woman had to be insane, but her madness was easily mistakable for a cool, rational, and unremarkable sanity, without any pigeonholes for the intrepid explorer to grip. Rodney could not and dared not attempt to anticipate her next movement or assume to glimpse into her mind.

"And you have never tried to seek them out?" Joy asked. Her tone was calm, almost bureaucratic, which disturbed Rodney all the more.

"Of course I did." Rodney could not stop himself from adding: "It's not like I've got the CIA behind me."

Gesturing with her gun, Joy shepherded Rodney into the house. Inside on nearly every surface was wood paneling coupled with a decor that favored rust and orange, leading Rodney to realize that his final moments would be staring at a 1970s showroom. As if sensing his fatalism, Joy casually said, "It's alright. I didn't bring you here to hurt you."

Joy invited Rodney to rest himself on an ornate wooden rocking chair while she faced him from a faded orange couch. Her dark eyes faced him wearily but with a seemingly superhuman determination. The atmosphere around them was that of an interrogation room.

"I'm pretty sure that you're part of the CLF yourself," Joy said, failing to hide her interest. "It makes the most sense."

Computer-like, Rodney's mind ran through the possibilities. Is she a detective? One that happens to take rather extreme measures? Was this retaliation? Were any of the CLF's antics even worth retaliating over? Aware that he was being scrutinized, Rodney made a valiant but failed effort at a poker face. Joy only smiled. "Close to the mark?", she asked.

Realizing he had no other reference point for this kind of thing, Rodney resorted to years of indoctrination through television and film. "And if you are?"

Joy shrugged. "Believe it or not, you just have to ask and I'll take you home. You can even call the cops on my own phone. I really wanted to... make a dramatic gesture. To show how truly interested in the cause I am."

Instinctively Rodney tensed, waiting for a trap. "You're kidding?"

"Not in the least. I've waited for... for something like this for a long time." To give her words the validity of action, Joy casually handed Rodney the gun and gave another shrug. Rodney, disturbed by the mere weight of the weapon, laid it down with an immature caution on the table.

"This is all..." Rodney started, but let the words hang frozen in the air. Was there any response appropriate for a situation like this? Of all the strange things to happen to Rodney in the last year, this seemed to be the most improbable. Confusion and fear ruled Rodney's mind and emotions, although deep inside a tiny yet growing part of him was proud that he had apparently inspired an apostle.

"I'm not afraid of prison. Not really," Joy said. "At least there I won't have to worry about finding a job and the money running out."

[AUTHOR'S NOTE: *This is an ideal point to describe Joy Chevern's past and how she came to be drawn to the CLF. It is true that she was from an upper lower class family and had a 3.9 GPA when she graduated high school. However, she was forced to forgo college when she refused to take out loans and could not find enough scholarship money. Embittered by the fact that her cousin who was a B-/C+ student managed to make it to college on an athletic scholarship, Joy became drawn to extremist anti-social philosophies. After a string of odd jobs with diminishing returns, Joy, by the time she confronted Rodney, was living in her dead grandmother's house and off a tiny allowance given to her by her parents. There she made a life of sorts out of perpetuating websites and e-zines promoting a radical and bizarre anarchist perspective.*]

"So, why are you interested in the CLF?" Rodney asked, recognizing that it was in his best interests to at least make Joy feel like she was being tested.

"The novelty– wait, that doesn't sound right," Joy said, shaking her head. "I guess there is really something new about them, not the same tired promises from all the socialists and anarchists. They aren't really promising anything, you know, and I think that's enough to make them totally worth listening to."

"Really?"

"Yes! I mean, the way they played the media over that whole Tammy Connery thing. They just made a joke out of the type of crap the media tells us we have to take seriously. You know, there's just something great about that."

Rodney wasn't sure if he should be pleased or concerned that someone had gotten so much out of his little pranks.

"What they're doing... it's like it's beyond any agenda, beyond postmodern," Joy continued. "And it's all happening here!" It was with that one term, with its solemn invocation of the prison that was Dead End, that Rodney began to feel some sympathy for Joy, but also a creeping understanding of how she might be useful.

"I'm not going to call the cops or anything like that," Rodney suddenly announced. He noted the poorly repressed relief on Joy's face. "In fact, I'll admit... that I do know a few things about the CLF."

Joy looked unsurprised but expectant. Rodney was still cautious. "Have you done anything... hm, political before?"

With that, Joy, after a hasty "Wait there!", disappeared into a side room and soon re-emerged, holding a laptop that was already showcasing a plain black-and-white website titled 'GOMORRAH UNDERGROUND.' "It's something I wrote," Joy said, a little nervous.

[*Since the Culture Liberation Front case became widely publicized, a number of fake websites and print pamphlets claiming to be the authentic Gomorrah Underground have surfaced, while the original website had disappeared. I have been assured, however, that the following is the complete and authentic copy of Joy Chevern's Gomorrah Underground.*]

GOMORRAH UNDERGROUND
A Genuine Testimony on the Incredible and Sickening Corruption of the Modern Western World's Elites

No one knows how often they go, but at least once a year some of the most powerful and wealthiest people in the world gather in Orlando, Florida. They go to a place, known among themselves as New Gomorrah, that is hidden in a massive complex beneath Disney World.

The general public knows absolutely nothing about either these gatherings or New Gomorrah. This account was found and posted on the Internet at great risk to the author.

Sometimes they congregate on Christmas or Easter, sometimes the day after one of their children's weddings, sometimes just on a pleasant summer weekend. Not all the world's rich and elite are among them on those special days, of course; it's only the ones who belong to an organization they half-jokingly call the Society of the Friends of Sin. Who belongs to this secret Society which even the most fevered of conspiracy theorists don't even guess at? The owner of the company that pumps out the corn syrup that poisons your body, the Senator who you actually think is on your side, the movie star whose half-naked promotional photos you jerk off to, and even your President and your Pope.

Before the bacchanalia, their agents, chosen for their professional discretion and their absolute trustworthiness, scour the world for the discarded and despised: homeless veterans and teen prostitutes, juvenile delinquents and the insane, gay runaways and Deep South Muslims. In the pristine biosphere that comprises much of the New Gomorrah compound, they set these people loose on the pristine fields, the emerald grottoes, the shores of the lakes and canals thick with exotic fish. Once these people have had time to cope with their confusion and fear and perhaps even form uneasy alliances, then they come on thoroughbred horses, dressed perhaps in aristocratic robes centuries out of date or in traditional fox hunting gear or in the military uniforms of dead empires. Their weapons of choice too vary from season to season. Depending on the mood or the chosen theme, they ride with rifles or with spears and swords. What never changes is that it is a hunt, a friendly little competition between peers, where the one with the most kills wins the day.

One time, my source—let's call him Smith—told me that they, still fresh to the games of the Society of the Friends of Crime, trembled and vomited at what was demanded of them. The one who comforted them happened to be a self-proclaimed and nationally praised man of God, even invited to speak at a President's invocation [*forgive me for not being able to use names; I assured Smith I would not*]. My source asked him how he reconciled what he preached and believed with what he had so gleefully done. It was inconceivable, especially since Smith had watched him as he cracked open the skull of a fourteen-year old drug addict, scooped off the streets of Tokyo, with the butt of his gun. The holy man only laughed and confided that he believed in no God but Nature. With the same tone he usually took with his sermons that promised brand new mini-vans and college funds and three-story houses to the humble and godly, he explained his real theology:

"What was done to that unfortunate girl was only unjust from her point of view. I assure you that from my point of view nothing could possibly be more just. After all, killing her gave me pleasure. There are two sides to every drop of pleasure, my friend. The pleasure appears cruel and unfair from the victim's perspective, but to the one who applies the pressure and receives the pleasure, it is as fair as possible. When one's emotions beckon, no matter the point of view of the one who will suffer, they are the call of Nature, the only true and living God. These feelings and the will to act upon them were bestowed upon us s by Nature, and if Nature leads us to commit what society categorizes as crimes, they are necessary nonetheless. Nature's motivations are indeed terrible and incomprehensible, but its workings are obvious. Those of us with no flair for morality have no choice but to succumb to the tyrant, confident that this tyrant is Nature and that we are delegated to work horrors in the world so that the harmony of the universe be preserved." Smith quickly learned that these were the guiding principles of all the members, and that they too would be expected to believe or else risk becoming a victim too.

Later Smith learned that the preacher had the child's body sent to his room, a revelation that by then they knew they had to laugh at. Smith spent the night trying to suppress his imagination, an aspiration assisted by his horror at learning over mimosas with the Secretary of State that the President enjoyed having pictures of soldiers killed in the latest Middle East war on him at all times, since he was not long on the job before he found that his power to send good, honest patriots to die thousands of miles away a wonderfully reliable aphrodisiac.

It was not even then that inspired Smith to make this revelation. Nor was it the next morning when he was invited to have breakfast with a member of Congress, who invited him to a feast of bacon, ham, fruit salad, eggs, pancakes, waffles, coffee, exotic juices, and hot chocolate. They ate at a vast luxurious table on fine china, while facing them in a dirty, rusted but still strong prison were a mob of people, taken away from some of the most impoverished regions of the world and starved for days. Over the fine banquet, the Congressman confided that the last time he felt sexually aroused was when he voted against granting additional emergency relief funds to his own district days after it had been struck by a catastrophic tornado. This did not quite shock Smith as much as learning that a Congresswoman famous for denouncing the destructive influence of homosexuals on youth had made for herself a private show where a Boy Scout troop, all the sons of her constituents, were brutally sodomized on stage by diseased male prostitutes gathered from the sleaziest slums across Europe.

None of these are what finally drove Smith to betray his kind, nor the murders and orgies that followed. Instead it was the closing ceremonies. The Pope had found the most faithful Catholic he could discover, a CEO celebrated in the media for both her savvy and philanthropy had brought one of her lowest-paid yet hardest working employees, and a government minister from Canada was accompanied by the teenage winner of a patriotic essay contest. Each one, exhausted and broken from various games enacted by the Society's members, was strapped nude to a giant dart board especially made for the purpose. They began a chaotic game with traditional darts but soon enough it escalated to arrows and then bullets, until all that was left of the loyal three was a mess of blood and pulp.

After he had told me these things, Smith said to me, knowing that he would die, and that he would not die well, that these are the true faces of the people who run the world.

"It's allegorical," Joy helpfully said.

In an instant, Rodney realized that this woman had to definitely, without doubt and without qualification, be insane. That thought was immediately followed by the pleasant revelation that she would also be useful.

In a moment as beautiful as any religious conversion, or indeed a lost soul finally finding its shepherd, Rodney took Joy's hands in his. When she did not move back, Rodney gently, paternally embraced her. "I think they'll be glad I met you."

7

A stiff Professor Morrison, while speaking to an off-screen TV reporter, said, "It is tragic that someone vandalized the entire Zmora exhibit..." he said, his voice flat and stale. The camera revealed that the portrait of the anonymous noblewoman had been de-defaced (although not without damage to the original, leaving glaring white marks around where the woman's right cheek and eye should be) and the authoritarian mannequin had "AVANT POSEUR" spray painted on its torso in hot pink. As gloriously, almost heroically uncommitted as Professor Morrison was, he added with just a bit of impishness, "... still, perhaps the vandals were making a statement of their own."

"The activities of the CLF have really crossed a line now." This time the camera was broadcasting the scowling face of the museum curator. Her eyes flashed with what might have been genuine anger or perhaps just a juvenile theatricality. "I just don't understand how anyone, no matter what their agenda is, could interfere with someone's message like that."

Rodney smiled over his laptop, where this week's article about the vandalism at the museum was already almost born, delivered by fingers greased by discount potato chips. No longer did he have to place himself so quite close to danger, and Joy could be relied upon to escalate the CLF's war on nearly anything that would make for good material.

True, she had started small, like Rodney himself. Students at Rivermont went to class Wednesday morning to find that nearly every blackboard had "THE BABY BOOMERS LIED TO YOU, YOU'LL BE LUCKY TO BE AN ASSISTANT MANAGER" written on it. But with no prompting from him or "the CLF" she had gone even further.

At first, when Joy had told him that she planned to vandalize the Zmora exhibit, Rodney felt that she was perhaps pushing everyone's luck to the breaking point. Sensing his reticence, Joy assured him that she would not say anything, if she was arrested. In fact, she swore that if worse came to worst she would make sure the authorities would be convinced that she *was* the entire CLF. Rodney hoped that it would not come to that, at least not just yet.

The next day Lucinda chuckled over Rodney's copy. "You really are too damn lucky for your own good. When I had your job, the best thing I ever got to write about was a Neo-Confederate parade."

"I think I vaguely remember that. I—"

"Christ," Lucinda blurted out. "Don't make me feel old. Anyway, I was sort of hoping that some fight would break out. Hell, I wanted a riot! Black smoke and dead bodies everywhere! No luck, though."

"I'm sure it was still an excellent excuse for a story."

"Yeah, well," Lucinda said, lighting up a cigarette right in the middle of the office. Tales of the CLF, it seemed, had emboldened her. "It did get a lot of people riled up, one way or another. That's the thing about journalism. People are always looking for an excuse to get mad, or feel righteous, or whatever, even if they won't do anything about it."

Lucinda did the little walk and the majestic hand gestures she always reserved when she was pontificating. "I don't really like talking about my sister. We just talk twice a year on Thanksgiving and Christmas anyway. She married a Methodist preacher who told me I was going to Hell the third time I had a conversation with him. Well, she always says that we're witnessing the fall of civilization, 'cause there ain't no taboos left and every last envelope has been pushed off the table. There's nowhere left to go except, I don't know, legalized rape and gladiatorial fights or something.

"You know what I tell her? Yeah, first I tell her that it's a bunch of bullshit. But then I tell her that every taboo that gets knocked down two more pop up. Sure, maybe deep inside or when they're feeling awful about the world everyone wants to be free and all be libertines or whatever, even if they wouldn't admit it if someone stuck a shotgun in their mouths, but even more than that they want things they can call sins or politically incorrect or problematic or whatever and look down on and get shocked and appalled by. It's what gets every culture going since the Hittites."

Lucinda put out her cigarette. "You can quote me on that, you know, when you write the book."

"What book?"

"Ha! Surprised you ain't thought of it already. A book about the CLF!"

A warm feeling echoed from his stomach to the rest of his body. The thought honestly didn't occur to him. He had been quoted by and was even working with national journalists on the CLF's activists, but he had just naturally hoped that some divine opportunity would present itself. To try to grab the nation's fickle, ADHD-ridden attention with a book, however—it was such an obvious idea, and yet Rodney had never been graced by it.

"Should I? I mean..." Rodney let the sentence die stillborn.

Lucinda cocked her head. "Yeah, I think you know what I'm going to say. I mean, it's one hell of a premise, but I don't know if you've got enough stuff to get through two chapters."

"For now," Rodney said, more to himself than to Lucinda.

Rodney was still debating over how to steer the CLF (and Joy) in the best possible direction for a book when he met Joy at *The Shire* over lattes. She happily shared that she had e-mailed copies of her *magnum opus* to every political student organization, conservative or liberal, at Rivermont College.

Rodney gestured to their current environment and the trickle of hipster Christians circulating around the coffee store. "How does it feel to be the author of *Gomorrah Underground* and be in a place like this?"

Joy shrugged. "It doesn't bother me any. I was

a pretty devout Christian when I was, oh, fourteen or fifteen."

"Oh?"

"Yeah. I gave it up when I realized that no matter what someone in the world believes you're going to Hell and, anyway, for most people sin is the only thing that makes them interesting. My parents, for instance. If you took away my dad's affairs and my mom's alcoholism, you'd just be left with a soda bottle collection and lots of bitching about Republicans."

Rodney nodded. "I guess I can understand. Isn't it an old joke that all the interesting people will end up in Hell?"

"I hate Hell," Joy said unexpectedly, and apparently loudly enough for the people around them to hear. They were ignored. "I guess I mean I hate the idea of Hell. People like Lou Meredith just get off on saying, 'Hey, those people you don't like and can't understand? Let me tell you all the reasons they deserve to go to Hell.' That's the only reason they have people listening to them, when you really look at it."

Rodney couldn't disagree. "What do you believe in now, if anything?"

Joy shrugged. "*Cogito ergo sum.* No reason to go further than that. Let me be surprised, even if it's Hell or oblivion. You?"

Rodney wasn't sure how to answer that. The religious visions he had were certainly a challenge to the lazy agnosticism he had adopted by default for most of his life, but neither had they compelled him to adopt any kind or creed or even definite position on the metaphysical.

"I guess I like to think we're all here for a reason," Rodney replied.

Once Rodney convinced Joy that the rest of

the CLF had decided to lay low but she should feel free to operate as she saw it, he visited Syd. They had kept up their visits on a tight schedule of once every other weekend, but recently Syd had without comment moved their timetable to once or twice every weekend. Rodney had been tempted to ask him what changed to bring about these increased visits, but Syd had resolutely discouraged such talk.

Another sign that their relationship had changed was that it was no longer about sex. Syd, who told Rodney that he once aspired to be a grad student in Philosophy until he realized he sorely disliked dealing with both students and faculty, had gotten into his head that Rodney sorely lacked an education on philosophy. This week the conservations were about Ludwig Wittgenstein's *Tractatus Logico-Philosophicus*.

Only after a lengthy conversation about Wittgenstein's general thoughts on metaphysics and language did Rodney ask Syd for his opinion on the book.

"Think the CLF would want a book on them?" Syd asked, as Rodney laid his head down on his stomach.

"I don't know," Rodney answered, arguably truthfully.

"Probably not."

"Why do you think that?"

Syd groaned, the way he always did when he was already bored with a conversation or train of thought. "'Cause once a lot of people know about them it's over."

"I think you have a point." Rodney let it end there and pretended to doze off, but he was meditating on Syd's words. Of course, Rodney had known since the start that his experiment would have to end. Not only that, but it could not continue for long. He knew that if he would succeed in making a name for himself it would not take long, and besides there was too much risk involved.

However, he had not counted on gaining an accomplice.

8

"It doesn't matter if they're Catholic, Muslim, atheist, Communist, anarchist, or capitalist. They don't give a fuck about changing the world, just getting enough people around to tell them they're not wrong" Syd said in a proselytizing tone.

Joy nodded, but with reluctance. "I guess I can see your point."

The three of them made quite the odd trinity: the false prophet, his stoic lover, and their mad disciple. But there was something serene about them, drinking bad coffee in a corporate bookstore and surrounded by students from Patriot University tricking themselves into thinking they were studying when they were really just engaging in the usual social rituals. At the moment they were probably the only people in the vicinity who took anything other than sex (or at least the Patriot University alternative, marriage, which essentially meant the same thing as sex) seriously, and yet there they were, extolling the profound seriousness of not taking anything seriously.

"That's what I like about the CLF," Joy said, giving Rodney a conspiratorial glance. She liked Syd from the start, but Rodney had convinced her not to entrust him with knowledge of her mission. Rodney assumed that Syd was sympathetic to the CLF, on the sound basis that he never grunted with annoyance whenever Rodney let the subject emerge, but he did not want to take any risks, not when he made it that far.

Rodney looked up from the draft of the third chapter of his book on the CLF, which he had so far titled *On the Home Front of the Culture War*. Syd had that particular look he always had when he was about to be contrary for the sake of being contrary.

"But aren't you holding the CLF sacred by now?"

Joy didn't seem fazed by the question. In fact, she laughed a little. "Well, maybe, but only as long as they respect the eternal now, you know."

Rather than let Syd force her into elaborating, Rodney interjected. "Where do you think they'll go from here?"

"I do wish they'd do something far away from this damn city, or try to anyway," Joy said. She had been in something of a skeptical mood since someone burned up the photographic exhibit of the Chinese artist smashing a Han dynasty vase in New York. She hadn't minded that it happened—in fact, she appreciated the whole joke of it—but was disappointed and even a little angered when Rodney informed her that it wasn't the CLF, but some copycats, who were apprehended by authorities just a week later and were sentenced despite their attorneys' ingenuous offense that it wasn't a crime, but social commentary, to vandalize a work of art that was itself nothing but a display of an act of vandalism. Joy seemed especially sour over the fact that of the two who committed the arson one had a trust fund and the other was on the verge of getting a MA from Columbia.

"Operating here is essential to their mission," Syd added. Rodney had to suppress a guilty smile.

"You're probably right," Joy said, finding refuge in her coffee.

It was a bit of a gamble but, seeing an opening, Rodney let himself blurt out, "All the more reason they can't go on forever. If they just stick to Dead End, it makes it especially risky to go on for that much longer."

Joy put down her cup. She still seemed surprised, even though Rodney with great caution had already broached the idea of the CLF folding up shop. "Yeah," she agreed.

Rodney decided to take what he hoped would be the final step. "Hopefully they'll leave something behind in the end."

"A manifesto," Syd thought aloud.

"Something like that," Joy replied.

Rodney had hoped from nearly the start that Joy would martyr herself with one last grandiose act of cultural madness, but now that he not only had a book but a top-name publisher interested in it he had to admit that the CLF had served its purpose. It would be better if Joy ended up in prison, content with sacrificing herself to protect the identities of the other members of the CLF, or lost interest herself. Instead she was taking risks. Just last week, she had in the middle of a conference at Patriot University personally presented to Patricia Liscord, the wife of an evangelical preacher famous for his very public meditations on manhood and traditional gender roles, a butcher knife and instructions on how to efficiently turn him into a *castrato*. Only the fact that Mrs. Liscord had no eye for a face quickly lost in the crowd saved Joy from possible arrest.

Later that week, Rodney met with Joy at her house, surrounded again by the decor of a long dead era. It was as official a meeting a fictional organization could have.

"I finally heard from the CLF," Rodney said, trying to avoid eye contact. "They still don't want to give either of us more information."

"Goddamn it!" Joy blurted out.

For not the first time paranoia surfaced in Rodney's thoughts, and he wondered how authentic Joy's impatience was. Regardless he went on. "Well, actually, from what they're saying they apparently think they've gone as far as they could. I've already forwarded you the e-mails."

Everything about Joy—from her heated glare, from the way she tapped her foot, from the curdled tone that deformed the vowels in every word—told Rodney that she was enduring a painful mixture of sadness and impatience.

Rodney decided it was better to plow ahead. "They wanted me to ask, are you planning something?"

"Oh." With that Joy gracefully opened reached under a couch cushion and pulled out a handgun, the very same one she had used to take Rodney captive, which she handled with an uncinematic casualness that for some reason disturbed Rodney more than anything she had done since the day they met. Rodney felt a chill; not because he sensed danger or he was intimidated by the presence of the gun, but because he sensed the escalation and he couldn't be entirely sure if he welcomed it.

"Are you going to kill somebody?"

"Maybe. I don't know. Does it matter?"

"For you, I'm sure." Rodney always knew that Joy would in the end wind up in prison—to be perfectly honest, he counted on it—and yet the fact that the inevitability loomed close enough to touch now gave him pause. Joy's passion, the poetic madness of *Gamorrah Underground*, her anger that defied simple political categorization; these things had sparked a curious and unlikely combination of sympathy and admiration in Rodney's mind.

Rodney tried a different track. "Listen, let me know and I'll pass the information on to..."

"I don't think they're real," Joy said. Rodney's heart fled to the soles of his feet.

"Not real in the way you wanted me to think, I mean," Joy added. "The CLF is real because they caused things to happen, and they caused me to take a step I never would have even thought about before. I've always been afraid to even illegally download movies, for Christ's sake! Of getting yelled at by strangers, much less being arrested! Until the CLF, until... you..." Rodney was so afraid that he did not even immediately notice that Joy was pointing the gun at him.

"You are the CLF, aren't you, Rodney?" Rodney did not answer. There was no need.

"I was never an idiot, Rod," With that, she gently laid the gun on the couch.

"It's okay, though, isn't it?" Rod asked. "Now you don't have to do anything else, and we can both get away with it."

"That's what you think?" Joy said, her back to Rodney. "So why did you do it?"

Rodney could only blurt out the first words his brain offered. "For fame, kind of."

Joy laughed, a musical laugh that was somehow untainted by bitterness. "So just the same reason for anything that matters."

Joy turned to him and sat down, as if she was about to give the news of a death. "Rod, I'm sorry, but you wrote us both into this story and now it looks like it's up to me to give it a proper ending."

"But we can do that now! I write the book and I split the royalties with you or... or something. We don't have to..."

"Did I ever mention my grandmother?"

Confusion caused Rodney to freeze, but Joy neither expected or waited for a reply. "Reverend Meredith reminds me of her. They both thought people should have their lives mapped out from preschool to the coffin."

Rodney sat down for the first time since he walked into the house where the two had first engineered their conspiracy. He had callously and without hesitation deployed Joy, but he had been used as well.

Joy glanced back at the gun. "What do I have to do? I'm going to launch a one-woman rebellion against something or another."

His conversation with Joy never left his mind, as he called his family to inform them that he was planning a vacation and even as he pounded on the door to Syd's apartment.

Rodney gave him no chance to react. "I'm leaving the country. Will you come with me?"

9

Rodney smothered the vague sense of sadness he felt as he stepped into the newspaper office, passing the front desk and the rack of newspapers and the framed photograph of some nineteenth century building whose relevance he had never bothered to learn. Rodney had some nostalgia not for Dead End or for the newspaper, but for the sense of struggle and the relief of triumph before it was lost, suffocated and left to rot under the massive weight of his fear. Still, even though urgency nipped at his thoughts, at the very least he felt he owed Lucretia, perhaps his only true ally, one last word.

Punctual in spite of his turmoil, Rodney had reported regularly into work. The monotony was a sure anchor into sanity. At the very least, Rodney could comfort himself with the knowledge that if he was destined to be arrested, being seized at the offices of the *Weekly Observer* was in its own way appropriate. It was a final act of defiance against Dead End itself, a total denial of the destiny that had previously been bureaucratically allotted to him. True, he would have no future, or at least no future worth anyone's casual interest, but at least it would not have been the future of a lower middle-class nobody.

At the end of the day, Rodney stepped into the back room. Lucinda was already there, illuminated only by the light of the sunset, leaning against an ancient wooden drafting board. She was drinking slowly, savoring a three dollar bottle of pale ale. Rodney suspected that his stories on the Culture Liberation Front had reinvigorated her, made her give half a damn about her job in years if not ever, but somehow she had sensed the subtle disruptions in the thin fabrics that tied his life to hers. It was not concern for him as much as the thrill of becoming part of something novel, something new, and now it was dissipating like a pleasant dream that had promised but not delivered the secrets of the universe. He knew all that, and respected it.

Rodney sighed and rallied his nerves. "Lucinda, I have to quit. And I can't give you any notice. I'm sorry."

To his surprise, Lucinda did not seem so shocked. "The hell, Rod? What happened?"

Rodney had prepared a dozen lies, all designed to soothe his own guilt. In the end, he did not use any of them. "I... I'm the one behind the Culture Liberation Front. I made it up, but I got this... insane woman to help me, but it's all falling apart now. I have to go while I can."

Lucinda stared at him, and still casually took one sip of her beer. "I suspected something, but not... so now what?"

"I don't know. I guess I have to leave the country."

Lucinda smiled, and without warning shook his hand. "You are the best journalist I have had the pleasure of ever meeting."

"You mean that?"

She smiled in such a way that Rodney was assured of her sincerity, and a little frightened of it. "In a world like this, journalism might as well be the last genuine art form." If he had a drink too, Rodney would have toasted that.

"It's why I really hate to think..."

"What?"

Lucinda, who was usually in the habit of staring one straight in the eyes, looked away to the unremarkable shelves of dusty, cobwebbed archival books, tracing stories of pennypinching town council debates and church barbeques all the way back to the 1920s, a bleak history that may as well have stretched out past the lifespans of civilizations and species and stars.

"Well, that you could end up in prison."

The idea had cruelly clutched his imagination with dagger-sharp pincers for a long time, but seeing it articulated even with just one word conjured up a heavy sickness in his stomach and made his pulse race and deprived him of all breath. He could hear Lucinda's voice, but only from such an impossible distance the words may as well have been static, echoing impotently across the voice. He had the sensation of falling, yet could not feel his own flesh. Even the basic concept of *falling* had been made abstract, theoretical.

The newspaper's back room had decayed around him

In its place he could actually see time thicken around him like a stew, the endless stretch of calendar days manifesting as gray, lumpy mud that opened before Rodney as if they were a malformed ocean. There were bodies there of all ages and sizes and races drowning in the gray, some stretching out their hands and some completely passive, but all sinking faster than any stone, never to surface again. They seemed to have no weight, and their minute gestures revealed despair and terror, yet they were silent, so silent they might as well have already been dead. There were other people floating above the waters, their faces warped by perpetual viciousness and contempt, descending upon the ocean to only drag the poor lost souls in deeper or to sadistically place their weight on them, making them drown even faster. They came in many forms, immediately apparent to Rodney: miserable husbands and wives; demanding bosses of mundane, poorly paying jobs; and parents, pastors, spouses and priests who hold tighter reins over other people's consciences than they themselves do.

Standing above this ocean was Lucinda, only she was dressed in white and blue robes, a vision of the Virgin Mary that was so pure and sanctified it must have been skimmed right from the daydreams of the Pope. Her bare feet touched the gray ocean but did not submerge in it. She reached out to Rodney, even though Rodney still did not feel corporeal.

"Poor Rodney," she said, but with a voice without the slightest trace of bitterness, so unlike Lucinda's voice. "You have seen Hell."

Rodney tried to speak, but he had no voice, or even an idea of his voice.

"You will face great hardships in the days to come, but you will triumph and you will ascend."

In a second, everything, including his awareness, shifted and felt solid and tangible yet again. Lucinda was grasping him. "Oh thank God. I would have maybe called an ambulance, if it weren't for... well, your possible legal troubles..."

Rodney slowly raised himself. His entire head felt as if it had the overwhelming urge to detach from his body and roll away. "What happened?"

"I think you had some kind of panic attack."

"It was..." Rodney began, but realized it was probably not best to lead Lucinda to the conclusion that he was insane.

"Rest here," Lucinda said, easing Rodney toward a dusty plastic chair, with a faded green luster that seemed to be resurrected in the magic hour light. "I'll get you a beer. That was my uncle's never-fail cure for a panic attack."

Rodney waited patiently, as if he was perched only in a chair in a doctor's waiting room, while Lucinda retreated to the mini-fridge further back in the recesses of the mysterious back room of the offices. Reluctantly, he began to realize he would miss this place. In a brief second, he found himself mourning for the future he might have had and never could have now.

His thoughts were dispersed by the feeling of old glass slipped into his hands. "Thanks," Rodney said, smiling at the woman he had seen as the Virgin Mary. It suddenly struck him how appropriate the vision had been. The Virgin represented salvation to the lost; so it was with Lucinda and him.

Much like a divine figure, she stood over him, radiating assurance and calm.

"You know, for what it's worth, Rod, no matter what happens and no matter how bad things get for you, I'm gonna write a book about you."

10

David's fingers were starving for a cigarette, the craving only sharpened by impatience, as he stood outside the austerely yet incompletely classical chancellor's office of Patriot University. Yes, conscious thought leashed them for now, but he knew it could not be for much longer. For as long as he could remember unhappiness, he had always hated the quiet but urgent necessity of *things*. It was that—not freedom from death or being sanctified or anything along those lines—which gave him hope for Heaven. At least, once upon a time it did. He didn't have any real hope in that anymore, but its ghost retained a foothold on his mind. The haunting was ever present, ever real.

He was free, however. Not exorcised, not properly anyway, but the faulty chemical plumbing in his brain had been a better spiritual instructor than a dozen Buddhas. His heights of mania taught him to appreciate the thrill of drinking even a mediocre latte just after narrowly avoiding a head-on collision with a drunk driver and the depths of depression revealed onto him the holiness of the flesh and all of its tiniest pleasures. He no longer felt he had God—or was it vice versa?—but he had forced himself to believe that happiness is his alone to achieve, not to be given to him. So it was that he went through the motions of belief, keeping his job as editor-in-chief and student manager at Patriot University's own newspaper *The True Patriot* and attending Rev. Meredith's church, but finding comfort anywhere but in gentle and sweetened suggestions of things to come.

He turned to the man on the cell phone, hoping he was done so he would have an excuse to shut up his mind for at least a few hours. Apparently he was a teacher that Rev. Meredith had turned his wrath upon, but he had been summoned back as one of those good will gestures that Rev. Meredith less than occasionally but more than rarely indulged himself in. No one took them seriously, naturally, but they never failed to make the true believers happy.

The ghost was always conjured when he wondered if it was worth taking paychecks from this man and his institution. He owned a piece of paper assuring the world that he had been taught as a journalist for about four years by Rev. Meredith, but he was bored with the pretense of trying to use the campus newspaper to seal up the cracks forming on the glass dome Meredith had built over his hearty and healthy students. Sometimes he thought his fingers would break out in blisters and tumors if he had to write just one more word.

"Sorry about that," the man, Mr. McKenzie, said with some kindness. "It was my girlfriend. She... um, didn't want me to do this."

David nodded. "It's okay." He realized he had no experience of Mr. McKenzie not being nervous, since the very second he had called him to ask if he wanted to give a follow-up interview and meet Rev. Meredith personally. It was all Rev. Meredith's idea, an attempt to counter the rumors all the liberal blogs were gleefully breathing life into that the good Reverend had cost a hard-working and well-meaning teacher his livelihood.

David abruptly added, "I'm sure my fiancée would feel the same way."

For the first time, Mr. McKenzie seemed at ease. "Yeah. But I was never really happy with how that reporter at the *Daily Observer* spun it. Seemed, I don't know, kind of confrontational."

David laughed a little, still high on his own audacity. "I think that's why Rev. Meredith liked it."

He realized that Mr. McKenzie was weighing him in his mind with the same timidness as a stray cat confronted with a seemingly kind human. "Do you like working for him?"

The question pierced David's brain. He buried deep his instinctive answer—*Not anymore*—and tried to conjure up something that was far more diplomatic. "Well, you know, I respect him, but it kind of feels..." David could see the waters of the Rubicon rushing from under his feet, but no longer cared. "...like all of this is for his benefit."

"All of what?"

"You know," David said, following with a theatrical gesture away from the building and toward most of the campus's east end. "But I guess not just the campus, but that huge church and having personal friends on the City Council and all that."

McKenzie looked shocked at what he was hearing, from one of the good reverend's disciples no less, but it was a shock that was mixed heavily with pleasure.

"I mean, I'm not saying that he's like greedy or all into ripping people off and all that," David said, believing most of what he had just said. "I guess I mean all of this wasn't just made for God or for his politics or whatever, but for him and what he needs out of life, you know."

Mr. McKenzie turned his head and let his eyes soak in the chancellor's building. "Sure. I think I can agree."

David had always contemplated how people like Rev. Meredith leave scars on the fabric of existence while most people amount to, at best, temporary blemishes. Still, one of the few loud and clear morals David received from his education came through the unlikely messenger of Professor Robert Sims's Comparative Religions class. Of course, this being Patriot University, the lessons the Professor imparted that any faith outside of Christianity lacked an essential ingredient that left them worse than flavorless. Despite the professor's best efforts, David learned that all faiths, whatever one thought of their generous metaphysical blessings, at least offered ways of appreciating life that didn't involve establishing large universities just for the children of your ideological fellow travelers or getting your name praised or damned on five different networks in the same day or whatever.

Sure, David was in one hell of a rut, one he might never get out of until they stuck him in the ground in an overpriced box. But he had a soon-to-be wife he sincerely loved and (he was reasonably sure) would love him indefinitely, and he had his health (apart from a tendency to have migraines on hot and wet days), and he had a comfortable life with every material need readily provided for (even if he hated the means by which he had to prove himself worthy at the moment of those material needs). Things were good, especially if weighed against the mud-soaked, back-smashing experiences of the grand stretch of humanity going back for miles to the musty, flooded caves of southern France.

"I hear you," McKenzie smiled, grateful for any tiny distraction.

"Well, we should go," David said, instinctively glancing at his watch. "He should be ready about now." McKenzie flinched at the sting of those words.

David sensed his pain and, like a slaughterhouse employee who approached their job with extraordinary sympathy and empathy, led McKenzie through the brightly lit and sky blue-carpeted halls of the chancellor's building to the office. Pictures of the reverend at various points in his career, usually involving victories of the pen and tongue against pornographers and sodomites and feminists, decorated the halls. It was like being in a museum dedicated to a still living man, who refused to just sink into the history books.

Reverend Meredith's office was palatial, with his own sixteen books given pride of place like any devout Muslim's Qu'ran. His desk always seemed clean of papers and notebooks, which always struck David as strangely infuriating, an insult to every single person who glimpsed it. In fact, the only decoration on his desk besides pictures of his children and grandchildren, which looked like they could have been cut and pasted out of a Sears catalogue, was a bowl of Skittles.

"David, thank you for setting this up," Meredith said, as always dripping with so much sincerity only the true believers could avoid the conclusion that he was insincere. McKenzie played his part by shaking the man's hand. That task done, he seemed to dissolve back into the shadows of the room.

David readied his camera, already composing the article in his head. Would he dare even imply that some people in Dead End were accusing the good minister of running a teacher out of town? The Rev. Meredith was only lucky that Mr. McKenzie was never a terribly popular teacher, if the cliched quotes like "He was always a great support" and "I always enjoyed his class" from his students were any indication.

"Well, let me take the photo first, and then we can..."

David's last thought before the bullet hit his head, and a small fragment of his brain ended up ruining a fresh bowl of Skittles, was that the woman who suddenly walked into Meredith's office looked upset.

11

Rodney always despised flying. It wasn't simply the unpleasant reality of being suspended in the air within what amounted to little more than a tin can. There was also the hollowness of the experience, of being forced to share essentially intimate space with dozens of strangers for an endless gauntlet of hours manifested in sweat and sleepless wrestling with tortuously uncomfortable chairs and the shrieks of toddlers. However, the few times Rodney had flown in his life he had been completely and truly alone. This time, he had a companion, who stoically refused to partake of any of the technological distractions offered in front of him.

Rodney did not really expect Syd to come.

Much less he expected for him to be sitting beside him, on the way to Amsterdam, that promised land for disenchanted Americans. Rodney chose Amsterdam on a whim, and because one of Syd's favorite topics of conversation outside secular teleological philosophies were economic disasters like the Tulip Mania of the Dutch Republic. Besides, Syd had a hatred of London that he would not or could not explain. Rodney himself had never been outside the United States before, and for some reason going to a country where English was not the majority language seemed almost safe, strong extradition treaty or no. Such details he would worry about later once they were safely ensconced in the cheapest place that wasn't a hostel reeking of pot and twentysomethings that had yet to be broken in.

"Alright," Syd had said when Rodney asked him to abandon his life because his lover was on the brink of becoming a fugitive because of a madwoman. When Rodney pressed him on the unimaginable magnitude, the ludicrous nature, of the situation, Syd shrugged—in that way where he used his only his eyes and face, and not his shoulders—and only said with the authority who knows and comprehends the essence of a pure mathematical truth, "I fucking hate it here anyway."

Rodney had not even tried to speak to Syd, except to ask him to stand up to allow him access to the aisle and if he wanted the extra cookie the stewardess had slipped him by accident or in order to bark up the wrongest tree. The sacrifice Syd had made weighed on him, and the burden was made even more backbreaking by simply how untranslatable Syd's thoughts were. Rodney did find a freedom of sorts from Syd's superhuman capacity for radio silence, but it was a troublesome freedom nonetheless.

"If I do go to prison, what would you do then?" Rodney asked out of as much concern as curiosity.

Syd was silent for an unbearable moment, and then shrugged and said, "I'll manage."

Exactly twenty-nine seconds later, Syd rested his hand over Rodney's knee as Rodney allowed himself to fall asleep despite the rigid defiance of his seat.

"I know you won't believe me, but this isn't just about you, or those two guys," Joy announced with heartfelt cheerfulness. "This is about my process."

Reverend Meredith was of course unwilling to enrage the young woman who was pointing a gun at the general region of his chest, but his vocal chords were exceptionally rebellious. "If you're going to kill me, just be done with it for both of our sakes." His left hand clutched the sofa cushion, marring it with sweat. Here he was, sitting in his kidnapper and likely future killer's living room, like a comfortable guest impatiently waiting to be served tea. "I'm sure it will take the whole afternoon to clean up all of my blood and brains. And it will take a lot of work."

Joy reacted as if the thought had never occurred to her. She leaned on the wall next to the entrance to the kitchen, holding her gun in so relaxed a pose it seemed like a natural extension of her flesh. "I'm not at all interested in killing you."

In spite of his own survival instinct, which was reasonably vibrant even though his last passing acquaintance with death was when he paused at an intersection where a car sped through the red light at 78 mph, Reverend Meredith could not hide the flash of rage he felt. His body shook as he said with painful effort, "And those two men? And the security guard?

Didn't you mean to kill them?"

Joy sighed. "I do feel sorry for them. I just couldn't let things get any more complicated than they had to be."

Meredith sighed, again trying with mixed success trying to remove the image of those two young men from his mind, their lives ripped from them by such infinitesimal pieces of metal and fire. Only the nausea that radiated from the very depths of his bowels up to his dry throat and his desperate mind kept him feeling real. He was learning that there was sanity in terror, much as Joy had already discovered that there was sanity in crime and cruelty.

"Is this torture?" Meredith asked.

Regardless of the less than pristine circumstances, Joy could not help but feel somewhat offended at Meredith's plain rejection of her hospitality. Her fleeting amusement at her own gut reaction was the first thing she genuinely felt all day. "What do you mean?" she asked, yet did not really wait for an answer. "Hold on a second. I'll be back in less than a minute, so don't think about running away. The car keys are with me. Plus the nearest neighbor's house is a little over two miles away."

In thirty seconds Joy returned with an open laptop, with a small webcam attached to the monitor, and some sheets of paper.

"Just tell me what the hell you want," Meredith said. "If it's a ransom, I can't..."

"Please don't demean me, at least no more than is necessary considering the situation," Joy said, absent-mindedly carrying the gun in one hand and making preparations on the laptop with another. "It's not about anyone's financial gain at all. Like I just said, this is about my process, and about making art that might change the world..."

With a dramatic click on the laptop, Joy turned to the Reverend and handed him, with flawless casualness, some papers.

Meredith weighed the word on his tongue. Art. He had only ever read and viewed and watched the things his teachers and later the critics and his friends told him he should read and view and watch, from *Gravity's Rainbow* to *Friends*. Likewise he railed against what the media told him to rail against, and hated what his instincts told him his congregation would hate. His first truly successful venture in the public eye was when he led a crusade against the film *Body Double*, and he took pride in the fact that a forty-three year old beautician and mother of a three-sport high school athlete wrote to him saying that she still had nightmares over his description of the electric drill scene. He recognized from almost the beginning that he too was a performer, a storyteller. There was no single second when he had any illusions about that. Now he was trapped in someone else's performance, and that knowledge made him afraid that he had come full circle. Like any great person who is damned with awareness that they are a great person, he dreaded any sign that the muses had become bored with him.

The grinding sound of a dying printer violently shocked him from his reverie. Joy had vanished again, only to reappear with a few more sheets of paper.

"Here's the script," Joy said, like a creative writing student eagerly showing her new work to a peer. Meredith could only take it from her with sincere solemnness. What else could he do?

*[Somehow the original script of **The Cog That Turns the World: A Film of Three Scenes** as written by Joy Chevern had been irrevocably lost, at some point*

during or immediately after police had first searched her home. The following is my own transcription of an online video that has been most authenticated by the available evidence, despite the dozens of imitations.]

FADE IN:
INT. AN OFFICE DAY
LANNY sits alone at a desk. He toys with a switchblade. Occasionally he plays with it like a child, pointing it at an imaginary figure. Sometimes, however, he holds it dramatically against his temple.

He puts the knife down. Moving slowly, he picks up a recorder and hits a button. He breathes heavily for a few seconds before he begins to speak.

                    LANNY
     Why haven't they kept me in the
     loop? I've been with the North
American Chapter of the Syndicate
   since I was recruited in my Intro
     to Sociology class by Professor
Proctor. I know I failed to organize
     the city riots that were supposed
   to coincide with the Revolutions of
   '89 but I... I feel like things have
     been going bad for a while now.

He pauses, considering adding more words, but instead he solemnly turns the recorder off and places it in the bottom drawer of his desk.

LANNY's secretary LAURA knocks and, without waiting for a response, casually strolls in.

> LAURA
>
> I'm going to get lunch. What do you want?

> LANNY
>
> I don't give a shit. You know it's just five restaurants in this town and that's counting the fast food. Pick for me.

LAURA pulls out a coin and flips a quarter.

> LAURA
>
> Tails: Italian. Heads: Chinese.

It lands on the desk. Laura gives a fast, sloppy bow in order to glimpse at the coin without picking it up. It's a gesture that almost seems to be mocking Lanny. However, Lanny is apathetic, not even acknowledging Laura's existence with his eyes.

> LAURA
>
> Chinese then.

> LANNY
>
> Fine.

Laura gives Lanny a look. She should

perhaps look concerned, but is clearly not.

                    LAURA
      Got any preferences? Speak now or
          forever hold your peace.

                    LANNY
                     No.

Laura leaves quickly. Only a few seconds after she leaves Lanny pulls out his recorder, turns it on, and begins speaking again.

                    LANNY
      Maybe the only question left to
      me now is if I should kill myself
      theatrically, in a way that would
      leave Laura gloriously traumatized
        for life, or get in my car and
        drive to the parking lot of some
      gas station long shut down. If the
      Syndicate has really abandoned me,
        then I might as well already be
      dead, although I hate saving them
                  the trouble.

Lanny retrieves his switchblade and again starts playing with it.

                  FADE OUT.

                  FADE IN.

INT. A HALLWAY

While carrying two bags of food, Laura
runs into Lanny, who looks determined
to reach his destination.

                    LAURA
        Lanny, where are you going?

                    LANNY
        Just running an errand.

                    LAURA
        But don't you want to eat first?

Lanny pauses, as if some profound
thought that otherwise would not have
crossed his mind in 200 years occurs
to him.

                    LANNY
        Why not? What's a half hour in the
                scheme of things?

Laura offers him a bag, which Lanny
accepts.

                    LAURA
        By the way, did you hear about the
        civil war in Azerbaijan? It was on
                the TV at the restaurant.

Lanny seems shocked, almost appalled.

                    LANNY

Azerbaijan? Are you sure?

                    LAURA
        Yeah. Did I pronounce it wrong or
                  something?

Lanny makes his way to the door to the
office.

                    LANNY
        No. I just thought it should have
              been someplace else.

FADE OUT.

FADE IN.

INT. THE OFFICE

Lanny sits at his desk, absent-mindedly
flipping through papers. Lanny seems
shaken.

              LANNY (mumbling)
        Azerbaijan. But it was supposed
        to be Brunei... I thought everyone
        agreed it should be Brunei...

Laura walks in, barely with a knock
as before.

                    LAURA
        Is everything alright? You barely
                  ate...

                    LANNY
It's fine. I had a problem I've been
working through for a while... now.
But I think I've come to realize
                  something.

                LAURA (quizzically)
                  What's that?

              LANNY (triumphantly)
  I've been under a... well, let's
  call it an illusion for a very,
very long time. But, see. There's
no driver, no engine, no struggle
behind history. Capitalism versus
Communism, freedom versus tyranny,
  imperialism versus human rights,
nihilism versus faith... it doesn't
  matter. No one knows what the
hell they're doing, no ideology or
  religion lasts longer than five
seconds without being subverted by
its own true believers, and everyone
will pick selling out over getting
                starved out.

                LAURA (bemused)
... Okay. So where does that leave
              us mere mortals?

For the first time in the film, Lanny
smiles.

                    LANNY
Drink and dance and laugh and lie.

In his book discussing the Joy Chevern incident, *Thou Hast Led Captivity Captive,* Reverend Meredith describes in perfect detail the experience of being forced to act at gunpoint. For half a chapter, he claims that he tried to use the switchblade shown in the film against his captor, although Joy Chevern to this day denies that the Reverend Meredith ever repaid her hospitality with violence. Nonetheless, it is the most popular scene from the CBS miniseries based on the book.

12

Inexplicably, less than a day after *The Cog That Turns the World* had finished filming, Joy Chevern had driven the Reverend Meredith back to his offices at Patriot University. He was released from her car into the embrace of a cold, bright morning. She was arrested just two hours later at a city park, casually drinking coffee and chatting with the thirty-six year old manager of a soccer camp who was thinking of leaving her husband (she decided to stay with him based solely on Joy's advice, or so she told a local reporter and two national talk show hosts). Within weeks, Joy went on trial and was promptly declared a terrorist and placed in a private cell in Greenville, Illinois.

Across the ocean Rodney and Syd had only observed the news reports on Joy's trial through the BBC like bit players in the drama. In the meantime, Syd had with unprecedented speed obtained a mastery of the Dutch language and gainful employment as security for the government. Rodney was not as lucky, and lived off coffee, pastries, and the sights of the tall, blond, and inexplicably tanned biking along the canal from his and Syd's apartment in the Jordaan district. Still, at least he could savor his notoriety from safety, as details of his involvement in Joy's crimes slowly unraveled.

Syd and Rodney also watched as Congress passed the Cultural Terrorism Act, which legally created an entirely new definition of terrorism that drew its inspiration from Rodney's own performances as the Cultural Liberation Front. It was the denouement of Rodney's own life's work, and while at times he missed his homeland, even Dead End, Rodney felt as if he had exceeded the ambitions that had long gnawed at his mind. He had inadvertently become an artist.

This all struck him one morning flush with orange and gold hues, as he returned from a bracing jog along the canal, made possible the second he no longer felt inferior alongside the Nordic giants who ruled Amsterdam. Whatever shape hands outside his view might mold his future into, at least the immortality of his name was finally guaranteed by the universe. Tragically, the universe did demand a price for its consideration, and it was exacted when, at the height of both his confidence and exhaustion, Rodney returned to his apartment to find representatives of the International Criminal Court. Just the night before, it was decided that he would be arrested and tried for committing crimes against humanity by helping conceptualize a new category of terrorism. It is unknown if any further religious visions had warned him of this development.

News of Rodney's arrest fortuitously reached the laptop of Lucinda Williams just when she was about to finish her first draft of *The Day Cultural*

Terrorism Was Born. After she had conducted a few moving interviews with the families of David Samuels and Terry McKenzie, she had quit her job at the *Weekly Observer*, an occasion she had marked by skipping her own going-away party. Still, she was grateful to the one person at the *Weekly Observer* who had helped her career transcend, and wrote him a sincere condolences card even though as she wrote it she was giddy at another piece of news, that she would be paid to lecture on cultural terrorism at Cambridge.

Reverend Meredith did suffer from a mild case of PTSD as a result of his ordeal, which he never quite recovered from. He was nonetheless very well compensated. Less than a week after the Joy Chevern incident, Patriot University received an anonymous donation of $1.5 million. Plus he could feel his sermons and his interviews with the media had been rejuvenated, all because he could breathe in a heady air deliciously rich with possibility and paranoia.

Even before all the hysteria over Reverend Meredith's kidnapping had died out, a second tsunami eclipsed not only the American press but the global community. Representatives of human rights groups lined up from New Zealand to Spain to defend Rodney Bauman from being imprisoned on the basis of a brand new and still weightless term like "cultural terrorism." Also there were many outside the United States who were not so pleased to see the United Nations so eager to follow the lead of the US Congress in chasing after this freshly spawned Cheshire kitten. In the end, after months of theatrics that thrilled the professional pundit and the average Philistine on the street alike, Rodney was sentenced to house imprisonment in a little one-story house somewhere in the suburbs of Utrecht. Rodney was not sure how to feel about this turn, but he was pleased to find that Syd, who had many strings to pull even after his short stint with the Dutch government, had managed to have himself assigned as Rodney's guard. To this day, they still live together under the auspices of the States-General of the Netherlands and the International Criminal Court.

As for Rodney's partner in crime, Joy still resides in solitary confinement in Greenville. In a rather perplexing gesture, she was nearly awarded an honorary degree by Oberlin College, but intervention by three Republican and one Democratic state senators prevented this. However, she has been commended even by the very conservative for writing extensive letters and blog posts to dissuade anyone from attempting to imitate her or Rodney. As of this writing, a three hour interview between her and Oprah Winfrey has been rabidly anticipated.

The End

Chad Denton is a writer and historian with a penchant for deviants and underdogs. Besides *Dead End*, he has also written *The War on Sex: From the Torah to Victoria*, which will be released in the Fall of 2014. He currently lives in Columbia, Missouri where he is finishing a doctorate in History.